"FIRE!"

He screamed. "What are you waiting for! Fire, Goddamn you!"

Edmunds' voice shouted: "Fire!" and the twelve-pounders crashed out. Their trucks rumbled on the deck like hollow drums, vibrating the fabric of the ship. It was all done smartly; Fox felt the black thoughts of mutiny impelled those sweating gun crews.

"Cock your locks! Fire—stop your vents!"

Again the broadside crashed out and the ship heeled.

But through the smoke an answering avalanche struck home. Fox saw a twelve pounder rear into the air and, toppled like a child's top, cartwheel across the next gun. Men were flung screaming. A cascade of splinters fountained from the mainmast and men at the guns clawed, as arrow-like splinters tore into them.

Then—from the waist, below the gangway, where a ball had struck home, came the shout most dreaded of all.

"Fire!"

The French had stoked their fires and heated their shot. Red-hot shot had smashed into *Duchess*. Smoke wreathed evilly above the gangway.

"Fire! The ship's on fire!"

Fox: The Press Gang

by
Adam Hardy

PINNACLE BOOKS • NEW YORK CITY

FOX: THE PRESS GANG

Copyright © 1973 by Adam Hardy

A Pinnacle Book published by special arrangement with
New English Library Limited.

ISBN: 0–523–00180–0

First printing, March 1973
Second printing, January 1974
Third printing, March 1974

Printed in the United States of America

PINNACLE BOOKS, INC.
275 Madison Avenue
New York, N.Y. 10016

CHAPTER ONE

Fox, second lieutenant of His Britannic Majesty's twelve-pounder thirty-two gun frigate *Duchess,* sprang up onto the quarterdeck to deal with the emergency there in time to see a nine-pounder shot take off Mr Midshipman Milne's head. The body still stood gripping the quarterdeck rail with whitened fists as blood spurted upwards ten feet into the air. Fox saw four distinct diminishing pulses as the heart continued to beat. The wind caught the plume of blood and swept it splatteringly across Fox's uniform coat and white breeches.

Amid the smoke and noise and ordered confusion of battle there was no time to worry about a dead man. Fox wiped blood from his face and cursed. A nearly-new uniform was ruined. That upset him. Someone would have to pay for that.

Captain Struthers shouted a command lost in the din. Smoke blew chokingly across the deck as *Duchess* heaved in the Channel chop. Struthers might be a gallant fighter but Fox had doubts as to his seamanlike qualities. The frigate captain had made no move as yet to bring the ship around; but the moment Milne's blood had blown across Fox that seaman's brain of his knew without need of calculation that the wind had shifted.

The French lugger heaving up and down in a smother of foam off their starboard quarter possessed sailing qualities Duchess could not match. Now, with the wind veering, they could let their head fall off and bring all their so-far silent larboard broadside into action. One controlled broadside from Duchess's twelve twelve-pounders and four twenty-four pound carronades should send the lugger to the bottom.

But Fox had not been summoned to the quarterdeck to command the ship.

The shattered wreckage of the mizzen topmast with its intestinal trails of rigging lay obscenely across the starboard quarterdeck carronades. The mizzen top-gallant flogged like a demented arm half over the side and the yards rolled and corkscrewed with every surge of the ship. Men sprawled in grotesque attitudes, their skulls stove in, their bellies crushed into red ooze, their limbs splintered. Fox could make out in the smoke and the writhing bulges of wind-blown canvas only five men still on their feet.

Fox pointed overside at the lugger. The wind was shredding the smoke away to leeward now. The lugger disappeared from view and then rose again and a row of smoke jets bloomed from her side to be immediately hurled away in the wind. Despite the gunfire the wind had not dropped but was clearly building up into a Channel gale.

'If we put the helm up we can—' he began.

Captain Struthers clamped his brass speaking trumpet to his lips and fairly howled.

'Mr Fox! Get that raffle cleared away!'

'She's ours if we wear now—'

'Mr Fox! Kindly attend to your duties as I direct!'

All George Abercrombie Fox could say was: 'Aye, aye, sir.'

The frigate surged heavily in the sea, heeling and corkscrewing unpleasantly, and spray flew inboard cuttingly. Smoke trailed away leewards. From time to time the lugger was completely hidden from view by the creaming green crests of waves that would roll remorselessly on until they broke on the rocky coast of France. Fox snatched up an axe and started in on the raffle. The men who had followed him from his position at the larboard side battery used cutlasses, axes, knives. Fox's short, chunky body balanced effortlessly against the violent ship-motions with all the expertise of a life spent at sea, and he was sometimes aware without any pride in the thought that the ship could spin completely around and stand on her head and he would continue to carry on with the task in hand without being disconcerted.

His left eye prickled him, and he resented this onset of a handicap over which he had no control.

There was no sign of Mr Beckworth, the first lieutenant, on the quarterdeck. Mr Savage, the marine officer, had been wounded early on and he was now below the cockpit lying on blood-soaked blankets spread over the midshipmens' chests, bleeding to death. And still *Duchess* had not worn around.

The axe bit into tarred cordage. Spray dashed inboard. Fox's clothes were stuck to his body by an unpleasant mixture of sweat, water and blood.

If he delayed, now . . . This dangerous wreckage half-toppling overside might act as a sea-anchor and pull *Duchess*'s head around by main force. Equally, the pendulum swing of a splintered spar-end might stove in the side to the sea. In the Navy you obeyed orders, come what might, despite the fact that in Fox's view all those givers-of-orders set in authority above him were bumbling incompetents.

He bellowed orders at his men hacking at the confused mass of spars and rigging, mercilessly sorting out the quickest way of freeing the mess and dumping the raffle over the side. A carronade had been pitched off its slide and a man's body had been crushed. As the mizzen top-mast slid towards the lee rail the body became entangled. It dragged along the sanded deck leaving a thick and slimy trail of blood.

Two of Fox's seamen—Huntley, the captain of number four gun, and his second captain, Leech— jumped in boldly among the raffle and began to slash at the entangling sheets, imperilling both their lives.

'Belay that!' Fox screamed through the noise of wind and the crash of the sea. 'Get out of there—

lively now! It's all going and I don't want two men I've trained up to go with it!'

The men looked up at him with water and sweat running on their faces, their eyes like coals. But they jumped free just as the last rope parted and the wicked mass of spars and rigging rolled over the corpse.

The carronade caught in the wreckage and pivoted, jamming itself, coradage whipped around it and the whole jumbled mass hesitated, lurched, hesitated again and then hung up. Masts and spars, canvas and sheets, heaved and roiled in the sea overside and thumped with a deep gong-like note on the deck, again and again.

Somewhere Captain Struthers was screaming orders. Fox, with his mind set on the object of getting this mess cleared away as soon as might be and resolutely pushing out of his mind the idea of turning on the lugger, ignored him. The glass must have been falling for some time judging by the way the ship was responding to wind and sea. This was hardly the weather to fight an action, especially against a saucy French lugger which could dance around them like a Spanish matador around a bull, and in only a few moments their chance to bring some semblance of success out of the sorry business would be gone.

The men were cautiously approaching the wreckage again and waiting for his orders, always ready to rely on his knowledge, however much they might resent him and his cocked hat. The splintered spars looked wicked, thrusting like boars' tusks as the ship rolled. Spray sleeted across Fox's face and he blinked and hardly noticed. Around the circle of vision of his left eye a pink and black halo was forming, lending a wavering air of unreality to the scene.

He spared a single glance for the captain. Struthers balanced on the quaterdeck clear of the raffle of wreckage, peering out over the humped seas at the bouncing spray-fuming shape of the Frenchman. *Duchess* still sailed hauled to the wind despite the loss of her mizzen tophamper; the driver was holding her head well up.

In the remaining time it took for Fox to leap in, judging his time to a nicety, and hack free the guilty rope, freeing the raffle to tear loose and topple overside, frigate and lugger had parted company.

The fury, the rage, the sheer frustrated anger boiling and seething in Fox made him strike the axe deeply into the last splintered spar as it speared upwards and pivoted overboard. The axe was wrenched from his grip.

The discipline learned in twenty-two years at sea reasserted itself. Surrounded as he was by titled incompetents, he had betrayed himself by his lapse.

With the inevitability he had come to recognise and expect in the Navy, he heard Captain Sir Grantley Struthers admonishing him.

'Mr Fox! There was no need to have lost that axe! The spar was free. Wilful loss of property will not be tolerated on my ship. It will be deducted, believe you me, sir, it will be deducted.'

Lieutenant George Abercrombie Fox had to say,

10

'Aye, aye, sir.' There was nothing else he could say to his captain, the Lord God Almighty on a British ship of war.

His impotent fury had now completely closed off all sight in his left eye. He stared around with both eyes wide open, but only the right eye showed him what was going on. By this time, since the unnoticed wound back in a half-forgotten fight, he was capable of carrying off his deficiency with aplomb. He could not afford to flaunt his handicap like a badge of honour as others, more loftily-placed, could do.

The French lugger was gone. There was no bringing her back now. No matter she was an insignificant trifle, she might have contained brandy, silk, tobacco—anything at all that might have brought in some prize money. George Abercrombie Fox was always in dire need of money—perennially, hungrily, and ruthlessly he sought for money. Prize Money for most seamen was a mere will o' the wisp; but it could come, it could . . .

Back in 1762, three years before Fox was born, the frigate *Active* and sloop *Favourite* had taken the Spanish treasure ship *Hermione* off Cadiz. The treasure had been fantastic, enormous, hardly believable. It had been sold for £544,648 1s. 6d. so one paper reported, another carrying the net figure of £519,705 1s. 6d. Either way, had Fox had the good fortune to have served on board *Active* he would have received a thumping £13,000 14s. 1d., and if on board *Favourite* an equally thumping £12,974 10s. 9d.

11

It could happen, it could.

No good could come of vain dreams. This captain of his had failed to do anything when the chance arose, and now the task of taking *Duchess* back to Plymouth must be faced. To be hoodwinked by a cheeky French lugger—that was what rankled! The wardrooms of the Navy would resound with laughter at *Duchess*'s failure. So Fox thought, bitterly, regretting his chance of plunging his fingers into a Froggy's money-chest.

Fox's ugly, pugnacious, cheerful face scowled around on the shambles of the ship. A rift of light was beginning to seep through into his left eye. Under the stress of action or fury or lust he sometimes lost the sight of his left eye, and if the danger or the fury or the passion were great enough his right eye also dimmed. That ugly cheerful face of his contorted in a scowl could daunt the horniest-handed old shellback afloat.

A ship's boy ran scuttling past him carrying a bucket of water which he slopped into the ready buckets standing where the guns' crews could slake the fiery thirst that seized men in action. The water might be filthy, blood-stained; still the men would drink it down, so maddening was the thirst engendered by powder smoke.

The boy was a skinny under-sized little runt of a lad, barely twelve, with a pinched face and protruding ears, and his bare feet left a trail of bloody prints. The blood was his own and not from a puddle into which he had stepped. He was filthy with grime and powder smoke, and down his cheeks

12

two snail-like trails showed the course of tears shed unheeding in the wearisome and terrifying ordeal of carrying powder to the guns.

'Belay that, lad,' said Fox. He spoke in a voice suddenly gentle, far-removed from his coarse and brutal roaring habitual to an officer urging on slop-hands and landlubbers and trying to knock them into seamen. 'We shan't need water on deck for a space. Get you below and tend to those feet—lively, now.'

'Aye, aye, sir,' the boy squeaked, overawed at being thus addressed so directly by an officer. Even by an officer like Fox. Fox killed the stirrings of a friendly smile. That was weakness. He would do himself no good if this boy fathomed how well Fox could identify with the horrible tribulations of a powder monkey. The boy would never understand that an officer who walked a quarterdeck with a telescope under his arm could ever have been a powder monkey like himself. To mention it at all would be toadying to the weakest members of the lower deck. Authority must be seen to have been in authority for ever and ever, amen, and so continue in authority for ever and ever, amen.

The boy scampered off on his bloody feet; but already Fox had turned his attention to the multifarious demands upon him. *Duchess* had entered this unexpected and quickly-developed action with all plain sail set and the wind force was now such that her top-gallants and courses must come off immediately before they blew to shreds.

The danger was imminent and real and yet at this

13

particular juncture only the captain walking the deck could give that order. Of the first lieutenant there was still no sign, and, of course, Fox himself was only on the quarterdeck by virtue of being summoned from his battery to clear away the mizzenmast tophamper cut up by the French chain shot that had done more damage than all the rest of the firing. An odd stray thought occurred to Fox. Mr Midshipman Milne had called to him on the captain's urgent orders. The last shot to strike had taken Milne's head. A fitting Parthian shot, that.

The carpenter reported to the captain, knuckling his forehead below his little furry Monmouth cap.

'Three feet in the well, sir. Making at a steady clip. Three shot holes below the water line, sir.' Macready, the carpenter, was a reliable man. 'I've plugged two on 'em, sir—but in this sea—'

Fox knew of that problem. The sea would be pouring in green through the shot hole, making a mockery of the carpenter's oakum-covered and tallow-smeared cone of wood, the shot plug. Hands to the pumps, then. . . .

Duchess had been sore hit—and all this from a puny pint-sized little French lugger with twelve nine-pounders and a couple of long eighteens! It was enough to make the blood boil in any true Briton's heart—and Fox was enough of an Englishman of his age, and a sailor facing the might of the Continent massed against Albion's Isle, to react in a predictable way at once chauvinistic and patriotic in the heady atmosphere of the times.

Mr Showell, the master, was now cocking his

14

eyes up at the pouter pigeon fore and main top-gallants. The motion of the ship indicated how she was bludgeoning her way through the seas which, grey-green and marbled with foam, rushed past in a tumultuous billow. Another hour and the sun would be down. And now the captain gave the necessary order at last and the crisp patter of horny feet on the decks, the twitter of the pipes and the sudden thwack of a starter laid across a straining rump told of the enforced discipline that could send men aloft in the teeth of a gale to claw their way out on the swaying yards and haul the stiffly intractable canvas in with blunted fingertips.

Refraining from consulting his timepiece to check just how long the evolution took, Fox carried on with his part in the preparations to restore order aboard. He took no delight in roaring orders, in berating laggards, in threatening floggings; but these were part and parcel of running a King's ship in time of war when men were scarcer to find than ice-bergs in the Southern Seas.

The lugger had done her work well. Lascelles, the surgeon, reported the casualties to the captain. Besides the ten killed and six injured—three mortally—at the quarterdeck guns, there were another nine killed and seven wounded by flying splinters or grape, received at the opening of the engagement when, for only the briefest of moments, there had been time for a decisive blow. Again Fox cursed savagely that *Duchess* had failed to get in that blow.

Captain Sir Grantley Struthers was a fair enough

15

captain, a fighter with above-average aggressiveness and spirit; most of his fellow captains would call him an excellent seaman—but in George Abercrombie Fox's book he was too slow, too indecisive, too unprofessional. As for the first lieutenant, the Honourable Charles Beckworth of the languid manner and the exquisite clothes and all the patronage of a titled father and friends on the right side of the House, Fox could never rid himself of the disgusting habit of wishing to spit whenever he heard the detested lieutenant's name.

Not that he would ever spit aboard a King's ship. Twenty-two years at sea had given him a healthy respect for the whiteness of a ship's deck. A single gob of spittle on that deck would be punishable, inexorably, by twenty-four lashes. Being the man he was, moulded by the Navy, Fox had no alternative but to agree that the punishment was just and fitted the crime.

The obvious concern of Mr Showell, the master, over the taking in of sail having passed and *Duchess* now thrashing along on her fore and main topsails and her driver and a jib, he could turn his attention elsewhere and now for the first time took close notice of Fox.

'God bless me!' exclaimed Mr Showell. 'Mr Fox, sir, you're wounded!'

Fox began to feel his arms and legs before he realised what the master meant, his own preoccupations having, as always, taken all thoughts of self from his mind.

16

'It's poor Mr Milne's blood,' he said. The formula was just right.

Of all the less than one hundred and eighty men left alive aboard the frigate perhaps only one, Mr Showell, the master, had a glimmer of liking for George Abercrombie Fox. Fox was accustomed to this situation. The master whose white hair testified to the years he had spent at his trade was a fine navigator and seaman and he respected those same qualities in Fox. As a consequence Fox had always been at pains to be polite to Showell.

He had also, through bitter experience, concealed his contempt for Harrison, the gunner. The warrant officers were a most important body of men aboard ship. Their good-will was an invaluable asset to an officer.

Fox's almost never-expressed but searing contempt for the incompetents among his superiors successfully alienated them, whilst the lower deck found him a conundrum and would never extend to him the respect they accorded unthinkingly to the popinjays who bought their commissions and who by influence manoeuvred through their examinations.

Fox was a loner. He always had been. He could see no reason why the future should bring any change. He could see no reasons and he did not care. So long as he stayed a commissioned officer in the Royal Navy he was a person who had a position and consequence—even, shattering to think, on half pay—with the result that he could bring in money for the family, and for his family he would

17

without the shadow of conscience lie, cheat and murder.

Gradually, as the Channel gale mounted and howled like a covey of maniacal goblins through the rigging, order was restored aboard *Duchess*. The bosun, Sullivan, the third lieutenant, Mr Edmunds and Fox set about rigging a jury mizzen topmast and yards. Whatever the pundits might say, Fox wasn't having his ship enter port with spars shot away in an action and not immediately replaced. That wasn't the way Fox had been brought up with Captain Cuthbert Rowlands. Despite the low company into which he had fallen since the war with France had begun four years ago, he did not intend to lower his standards now.

The captain received reports, and nodded, and paced what he could of his quarterdeck, and looked at the sky, and rapped out orders from time to time. He had come to rely on Fox, had Captain Struthers, rather more than he realised or relished. Now the great machine that was a frigate under sail hummed with ordered activity. The jury-rigging of the mizzen topmast would finish after dark; but Fox was quite right. *Duchess* was a smart frigate, and Captain Sir Grantley Struthers would keep her that way.

At last—at long last—Mr Beckworth, the First, the Honourable Charles Beckworth, stepped on deck. He had a bloodied rag tied around his forehead and his face showed the whiteness of a rat's belly. Fox looked at the bloody rag. He was a gambling man, when the odds were right, and he'd have

18

bet a year's pay that the blood staining the rag had never flowed through Beckworth's aristocratic veins.

'Demned hot work, that,' said Mr Beckworth, waving one hand airily. 'I see the Frenchy got away. A pity I was wounded and had to got below, demned pity.'

He saw Fox staring at him, pausing in the work of rigging the topmast. 'I say, Mr Fox. You'd best look sharpish about rigging that mast. We're on a lee shore here.'

In the normal course of events sending up top-masts was an evolution that should never take more than about fifteen minutes, and preferably far less. In the present case, though, the lugger's shot had damaged the mizzen top and Mr Macready and his mates were aloft, chipping and shaping to fit the new mast. As to the lee shore . . . Now, for the first time, Fox saw a glimmer of reason for Captain Struther's refusal to wear before the wind. But the French coast was at least five miles off, there was plenty of searoom. Fox could trust his own seaman-ship to know when a lee shore was potentially dangerous, as opposed to being an imminent danger against which immediate steps must be taken. But Struthers would know that his word as a frigate captain would be taken; the lugger could sail where *Duchess* would ground.

The gale seemed to have reached its peak; the ship moved easily enough and all unusual dangers had passed. Now there were left only the ever-present perils of the sea. Fox thought of that eighteen-pounder shot hole below the water line and grimaced. They'd reach Plymouth all right. As for the Honourable Charles Beckworth, that dandy could fall overside for all that George Abercrombie Fox could care.

CHAPTER TWO

Weak May sunlight glinted off the waters of the Hamoaze. Smoke from the tall chimneys of the biscuit bakery floated idly into the morning air. Men were at work in the dockyard and victualling yard and they would be hard at it in the rope walk and the mast house. The sheer hulk was being shifted out to place fresh masts in *Tremendous* whose nettings overside and flock of wherries and boats alongside as much as the garlands in what standing rigging she had left indicated her status. Here laboured the nicely calculated machinery of one of His Britannic Majesty's dockyards that kept and maintained the mightiest fleet the world had ever seen. Here, too, lay *Duchess* busily at work repairing her damage with the guard boats ceaselessly rowing and the marines on watch to prevent a single man from running.

Shore leave, of course, for the lower deck was unknown.

There was a change in routine. A cutter had

pulled out to them and a smart young Commander had vaulted aboard *Duchess* and gone at once to the aft cabin where he had remained closeted with Captain Struthers for upwards of an hour. Rumours swept the ship. Beckworth irritably reprimanded a careless seaman with a volley of filthy oaths delivered in his high-handed style. The men understood that. Beckworth, Fox saw, was needled that he had not been included in whatever discussions were going on.

When the Commander, very curtly, bade them goodbye and went down the side into his waiting boat, Fox thought that Beckworth would burst.

He felt confident enough the news had nothing to do with their ludicrous encounter with the French lugger. The butcher's bill for that maladroitly handled affair was more than that often suffered in a full-scale frigate action.

Only this January Sir Edward Pellew in *Indefatigable,* a forty-four gun frigate, in company with the thirty-six gun *Amazon,* had fought and run aground the seventy-four *Droits de l'Homme.* During the more than twelve hour action *Indefatigable* had only nineteen men out of 330 wounded. That was the sort of sea action Fox understood.

When Struthers summoned Beckworth, Fox, who now that the ship lay in port would not stand a watch, fretted over this hiatus. He wanted to go ashore and see if he could stretch his attenuated credit to cover a new coat. The blood had been washed out as well as might be; but his wardrobe was in a deplorable state.

Then it was his and Edmunds' turn. In the aft cabin with the marine sentry at the door removed to a distance of three discreet yards, Struthers sat at his table with a face as grave as any Fox had seen him wear. Beckworth was excited, wrought up, his handsome face flushed and his thick red lips pouting with anger.

'From the highest yard arm!' he was saying vehemently as Fox and Edmunds entered.

'Kindly moderate your tone, Mr Beckworth,' Struthers admonished him. 'This is a matter of the highest confidence.'

What he then said bewildered Fox for only a tiny fraction of time. But almost at once Fox saw with a clarity these officers could never achieve what they were really saying. The word was simple, brutal, and ugly.

Mutiny.

Over at Spithead the Channel Fleet had mutinied. It had all been done with decorum, in due form, with the men organised so that no one could say for certain just who were the ringleaders. Unpopular and harsh officers had been dismissed. The men's demands were being studied. Earl Spencer and a party of admirals had listened to the men's grievances, the King had granted the pardon they requested, it was all going well, apparently, then some titled ninny in the House of Lords had upset everything. Now the mutiny had sparked up again with a savage fight on *London*.

Admiral of the Fleet Lord Howe, the victor in the famous Glorious First of June, just three years ago, and now aged seventy-one, had been hurriedly sent to Portsmouth with *carte blanche* to unravel the mess. But the infection could spread. The Nore could explode at any moment. Plymouth should be sound—but . . .

'And, gentlemen, we are under orders to put to sea as soon as our passenger arrives on board.'

'Passenger, sir?' said Fox.

Struthers ignored him. That was his privilege as captain. 'We are chronically undermanned,' he went on, ignoring also, in Fox's view, the root cause of that shortage of crew. 'We need at least another fifty men—we can manage with thirty landsmen but we need twenty seamen.' He made a face that revealed a weakness to the watching Fox. 'The guardship can offer us only a handful, and as this damned mutiny could cause problems we must fend for ourselves. I have all the necessary warrants, signed and sealed and dated.'

Fox felt his lips close tight and his teeth shut together. It was coming. Beckworth might be given the task of bringing off the guardship's pitiful wrecks, and scrape up another gang of Billy Pitt's Quota Men, but he, George Abercrombie Fox, would be given the man's job.

Press Gang.

'Mr. Fox, see to it that you take the most reliable men. I leave it to you. Mind—I need at least twenty seamen among those you bring in. And the more landsmen the better. Mr Sullivan will be able to make something out of anything—God knows, he's had enough experience.'

24

That, Fox knew, was true.

Fox left to make his arrangements. For him there was only one bright spot. The men he would—find—would come directly aboard *Duchess* and so would be spared the dreadful ordeal imposed on them by the Impressment Service. They would miss the press room, and the fleet receiving ship—the slop ship—and then the fleet receiving-station where they would be regulated. Fox had once had the misfortune to be pressed and had gone through that awful route. He knew. And he had been a seaman trained, not a landlubber torn from a shop or a mill or a mine, completely ignorant of the ways of the sea.

The best men were taken from the ships of incoming convoys; but the tenders cruising the Channel would have picked up all the likely men long before *Duchess* could put her nose in. The whole business was a pigsty; but George Abercrombie Fox was a pig in that sty and he must obey the orders of his superiors. This was the way the Navy obtained crews; this was the way the Navy had *always* obtained crews. Pitt's Quota Men were in a fair way to demoralise the Navy—no doubt this mutiny had been instigated by some sea-lawyer swept up by the Quota Act.

He chose his men with care. Mr Sullivan, the bosun, must go with him. His muscular arms had knocked down more unruly sailors than he'd had hot dinners. Mr Harrison, the gunner, despite Fox's low opinion of him as a gunnery expert, could hit a frightened boy over the head with a billy as well as the next man. For the rest, all petty officers, plus young Samson, the smartest topman on the ship. He had a smart brain as well as nimble feet.

The law regarding Impressment was in theory strict; but like everything else when custom and necessity wore away the sharp edges, the law was constantly evaded. A Commissioned officer must head a gang, which must have warrants in due order, signed by a magistrate. Fox would have liked to have taken Mr Midshipman Lunt; but he was rowing guard duty around the frigate. Lunt had almost recovered from the shock of his friend Milne's death. He could not be spared his duty; he and Edmunds and Beckworth had to make sure *Duchess* remained in ideological quarantine. If mutinous ideas got aboard . . . A whole fleet, useless in time of war, was a terrible thing to Fox. He trembled at the thought of French glee, and the three deckers creeping out of Brest and l'Orient to fall upon a supine England. There would be no mutiny aboard *Duchess,* Fox swore that, as much by his own faith and memory of Captain Cuthbert Rowlands, as by his sense of fitness aboard his ship.

Sullivan was swinging out the launch amid a hoarse barrage of orders and yells. Men were decently at work about the deck. Gulls wheeled and circled in the morning air, their harsh cries cutting through the man-made noises. Wherries and other small boats plied the waters. Strange to think of what was going on in other parts of England at this time; of the sullen seamen battened in their ships, of the soldiers gathering, of the heated exchanges among the politicians, and strange, too, to think that even now on land there were men going about their business unknowing that on the morrow they could wake aboard a King's ship bound to serve the Navy under the lash and the merciless discipline of the service.

Fox had no real compunction for them. The nation was at war and a man's duty called him to fight for his country. If he was pressed to go to sea, then he merely took an unfortunate method of getting to a place where he could be of use. He might as well 'list for a shilling. And, the clinching argument, trained seamen were needed to sail *Duchess*. Captain Struthers wanted them and he had sent Fox to obtain them. If Fox failed, then any small hopes of promotion he might have, consequent on an act of supreme valour and courage and foolhardiness, would vanish forever.

When all was ready Fox went aft to report to Struthers. A wherry rowed by two fat and blowsy women hailed by the watch responded with the 'aye, aye' which indicated an officer was aboard. Fox paused as a young man leaped for the chains and dragged himself on deck.

He was trim and dapper, with sleek yellow hair and a thin aristocratic nose. His midshipman's uniform showed a glory of newness, making Fox's cold coat look its filthy drab self by contrast.

'Mr Haines reporting aboard, sir,' this apparition said stiffly to Fox.

'Well, Mr Haines,' said Fox, grimly. 'You'd best cut along and report yourself to the first lieutenant.'

27

'Charley Beckworth,' said young Haines, his smooth face showing a natural superiority. 'My cousin. I'll cut along, then, Mr—ah—Mr—?'

Fox did not enlighten him but turned and bellowed with so ferocious a tone that a passing ship's boy scuttled to the other side of the gratings.

'Mr Sullivan! Kindly lay that raffle out as I expect to find it in a King's ship! Have those ropes flemished down before we cast off!'

'Aye, aye, sir,' came Sullivan's answering bellow and then his hoarse voice shouting abuse at the watch and his rattan thwacking down emphasised his immediate carrying out of orders. Fox turned back and watched Mr Milne's replacement trot gently up the deck and disappear below. That young middy had been aboard before. No doubt—in fact without any doubt at all—Beckworth's influence had had him posted to the frigate out of some line seventy-four. All middies wanted to serve aboard saucy frigates. It was what came of reading broadsheets and listening to popular songs. The saucy *Arethusa* had much to answer for.

Captain Struthers did not delay Fox long. He gave him the warrants, made sure he understood what was wanted, and then set about tallying up the wine list he was preparing to stock his private wine chest.

The launch pushed off and the oars drove deep. That meant the guards boats would be that much more hard-worked to do their job without the largest boat belonging to the frigate to take a tour. Edmunds waved from the cutter as Fox passed. Fox returned the greeting perfunctorily. Edmunds was a capable officer; but he needed to be led and given instructions at all times. In Fox's view Edmunds stood even less chance than he did himself of reaching post rank.

Pulling steadily the launch cleared the Hamoaze and East Stonehouse showed ahead with Cremyll to starboard and there was time now to order the oars inboard and set the masts. Fox watched that all was done spick and span. The mast was launched aft and the upper pin was clamped, then the forestay, one end of the main tackle was hooked to an aft eyebolt, the head of the mast was lifted by a thrusting forest of brawny arms and then the main tackle could be heaved. Fox used two backstays led forward on either bow to increase the lift and steady the mast. The moment the mast was upright the lower pin was rammed home and in the next moment the shrouds were set up and the sails were readied.

Fox made sure in his grim authoritarian way that the throat halyards were well up; he knew that many eyes would be watching the launch from *Duchess*, and a few telescopes would be trained on her. Those watchers might guess for what purpose she so brazenly sailed out; but also they would be noticing every aspect of the boat, her trim, her neatness and, particularly, the way her sails were set. In the nature of things a rope's end trailed over the side at the end of the manoeuvre, and Fox roared viciously at the nearest man to haul it inboard and stow it.

They picked up speed now with all sails set

creaming past the buoy and heading out across the Sound. Again Fox checked that the set of the sails was just as he wanted it. The luffs of the sails were hauled taut by bowsing down the tacks. So, almost unthinkingly, did George Abercrombie Fox take his little command out on a raid on the manhood of England.

His understanding of the wind and weather was quite automatic; at any hour of the day or night he could judge his actions in conformity with the weather conditions without conscious effort and he sometimes wondered if he could do this when he was asleep. Certainly, to the man who had sailed *Invulnerable* through rocks and shoals where a frigate and a sloop had ripped their bottoms out, sailing a launch across Plymouth Sound and along the coast could be done almost in his sleep.

Now he had chance to think and plan. Privacy aboard a frigate was virtually impossible except for the captain and now, when sitting in the sternsheets of the launch Fox might have lapsed into himself and given himself up to contemplation, he thought of his mission. Certainly a shivery little memory of his childhood on the Thames returned to him as he sent the boat skimming over the water. From his earliest recollections he had been in sailing-boats, sailing sailing-boats, mending sailing-boats. As a tiny child he had spent hours on the Thames marshes hunting the enormous flocks of wildfowl. He was an uncanny marksman with a sling and, even today, he habitually carried with him a discreetly folded black kerchief. That kerchief had done good work with pebble, musket ball or lead weight before now.

As darkness settled in he steered in for Walsend Bay. A few scattered lights from the fishing village reflected on the calm surface of the water. The launch grounded with a muffled grating and at once the men sprang out and ran her up a few yards on to the coarse gritty sand. All orders were given in whispers. The men formed up carrying their bludgeons and dark lanterns, Fox put himself at their head and they set off into the darkness.

Fox had seen to it that every man had eaten before beaching, and the extra barricoes of water he had had put into the launch would be broached well and truly before this night's work was done. They ascended a stony path with the wind whipping the bushes on the landward side. Above them cloud masses obscured the stars. The moon would be up in about three hours; nice timing, Fox considered, all things considered.

What Captain Struthers had ordered him to do was in reality an impossibility. There were no prime seamen to be had, at this day and age in the history of the war, just hanging around on the coasts of England. The Impressment Act stated that no one should be pressed under the age of eighteen or over fifty-five. What the government attempted the Navy was forced to circumvent to fill its ships by trickery. Fox, too, would be forced to act illegally, in the eyes of those who were not responsible for the defence of England.

They skirted the fishing village very circumspectly and marched on inland. Gradually the scenery of the countryside changed, leafy lanes deep sunken against the west wind, the soughing bulk of trees above their heads, the lonely lights of isolated farmhouses, all told them that they were leaving that narrow coastal strip of land where a sailor felt as much at home on land as a sailor ever could.

With halts and regulated marches, they reached the outskirts of Candale. Here they lay in wait. Candale had one thing to recommend it to Fox; it was a small market town. That meant farmers, labourers, hard men of the soil, coming in to get drunk.

As the farmers and labourers wended their drunken way home they were snapped up. A savage blow on the head quietened them, one by one. Fifteen blows later Fox considered he had enough of these landsmen. Now he could see about the really difficult part of the operation.

'March 'em down to the beach,' he ordered Mr Sullivan. 'You know what to do to keep 'em quiet. Meet me at the village as soon as you can—and quietly, mind.'

'Aye, aye, sir,' said Sullivan. He thwacked his cudgel into his hand. Fox wondered which was hornier or harder, cudgel or hand. 'They won't give no trouble, sir.'

There was in Fox no distaste as there was no liking for this job. It was something he had to do. If he did not do it efficiently his head would roll. Struthers would see to that, just as he would see Sullivan was disrated if he failed.

The quietness of the night breathed around them

32

as they settled down just outside the fishing village to keep observation. Fox had discarded any ideas of breaking into the houses. It had been done—God, yes, it had been done!—but that wasn't a subtle enough way for George Abercrombie Fox. It would raise an alarm, and that would destroy his chances, given the small number of men at his disposal.

Sullivan had rejoined him by the time the first streaks of light showed in the sky. The men were rested. Now they waited near the drawn-up fishing boats and the nets hung out like spiders' webs. Sounds reached them from the village. Voices, the occasional laugh, the slam of doors, and then the trudge of feet on cobbles. The men tensed up, their knuckles whitening on their cudgels. Fox remained calm. He had to choose exactly the right moment; there was a great deal at stake here.

The fishermen had reached their boats now and were throwing gear in, cracking coarse jokes, scuffling their feet in the shingle. Tackle groaned. 'Just twenty,' Fox prayed. 'Just twenty. It's not much to ask.'

Dawn was whitening the beach now, sending streamers of light across the sea. The fishermen began to tail on to their boats, all helping to run out a boat at a time. Fox waited. His breath came just as evenly as it did when he walked the quarterdeck on watch, or awaited the smashing stroke of a French seventy-four's broadside. He half raised. His men were all looking at him. He saw the hungry look on Mr Harrison's face, and that had no power to revolt him.

'Right,' he said, very softly. He stood up. He opened his mouth to give the order when he saw the boat standing in to the beach. His brows crinkled. Shown up by the horizontal light, hard and etched, men crowded the boat. Sailors, men armed with cudgels, savage-faced men, led by a Lieutenant with a great deal of gold lace about him, a rival press gang leaped ashore with fierce and venomous shouts, began to hunt down the fishermen Fox had so patiently hunted.

CHAPTER THREE

Instantly Fox let out a fierce bellow and charged.
He led his men in a dead run for the bewildered knot
of fishermen. Now the rival press gangsmen were
leaping out of their boat into the water, racing up
on to the beach.

Among the fishermen a great hulking man stood
out head and shoulders above the others. His black
hair curled in crinkles all over his skull, and his
swarthy Cornish features showed comprehension of
his danger and immediate savage challenge. He gave
a yell and began to run back to the village followed
by the other fishermen.

The two parties collided head on. Fox got in a
blow and was struck on the shoulder. He reeled
back and saw Samson, his smartest topman, hacked
down and Harrison, rising bull-like in the mêlée,
smash two heads together. Fox dived, grabbed Samson's collar, hauled him up. Sullivan was methodi-
cally knocking men over. For a few moments it was
all cut and bash, with men yelling and reeling over

35

the shingle, the sound of bare feet seeking for purchases, the shrieks of men savagely chopped off as cudgels struck home.

The huge black-haired man brushed off two petty officers as though they were mere flies. His face showed all the violence of elemental fury.

'Certificates!' he was shouting. 'Exemption!'

Sullivan tripped a running man, cudgelled him face first into the shingle. The bosun started towards the giant. 'I'll stificate you!' he roared.

Fox could not hear that. He could hear well enough; but he *must* not hear. He covered the situa-face first into the shingle. The bosun started to-him away. The sailors from the boat were now perilously near.

'Avast that!' he yelled. 'Bring what you've got! Jump to it! Lively!'

His men were slinging insensible bodies over their shoulders and padding back along the beach, heading for their own boat. Samson was running a youngster along with an arm twisted up his back. Harrison and Sullivan circled the giant warily and Fox saw quite clearly that their professional instincts had been aroused. Once tamed the giant would be worth two men at the capstan or the pumps.

Fox saw the giant reach into a pocket of the jumper he wore and, as though that was a preconcerted signal, the two *Duchess* men leaped for him. Blows rained down on him. He tried to lift a hand and he was brutally battered to his knees. Harrison had his fist closed around the giant's arm, keeping his hand thrust into that pocket. Sullivan kicked the giant's legs from under him. A flurry of blows and then the two warrant officers could snatch up the Cornishman and bring him along bundled between them like a rolled hammock.

They'd never make the boat in time. Fox gasped out his orders. A ragged rear guard formed. There could be no chances taken now. The gold-splattered lieutenant at the head of his men came plunging and sliding up the shingle. Fox turned to meet him.

'Too late, I think,' he said, putting coldness and formality into his tones.

The lieutenant checked. A burly man at his elbow, his bosun, probably, looked angry and sullen, ready to dash on. But Fox had sized up his man. A few cudgels slapped into meaty palms behind him.

Every minute gained was a minute towards victory. Still the lieutenant hesitated. Then, when he spoke, Fox knew he was that much more towards success.

'Lieutenant Cathcart, *Thunderer*,' the officer said, speaking stiffly. 'To whom do I have the honour of speaking?'

'Lieutenant Smith, *Tremendous*.' Thank the God of sailors that he'd remembered *Tremendous*, dismasted, garlanded, soaking on the Hamoaze!

'I think those men will carry certificates of exemption.'

Fox kept his face straight. So the fool, beaten, was pointing out an illegality he had been himself about to commit!

Here was Harrison, black and burly at his side.

The gunner's cudgel smacked up and down into his palm.

'Did you find any certificates of exemption, Mr Jones?'

Harrison understood. 'Nary a one, sir, Mr Smith.'

Fox let a steely little smile play about his lips. He used the expression carefully, when it would do the most good, chilling a man with the terror to be inflicted on him by the awful authority of the Navy. 'No exemptions, Mr Cathcart, you see.' He jerked his head. 'If you wish to put the matter to further arbitration, I think I can accommodate you.'

Cathcart's bosun surged forward and Harrison, as though meeting some primeval challenge, reared forward in his turn.

For a moment the issue hung. Then Sullivan came running up. He opened his mouth, shouting: 'All safely aboard, Mr Fo—' when Fox roared over the bosun's voice: 'Thank you, Mr Brown. Prepare to shove off.'

He looked back at Cathcart. The man looked crestfallen. Fox nodded his head towards the village where black-shawled women appeared, running, bare-headed and bare-footed, for the beach. 'You may take your pick of what you find there, Mr Cathcart. I bid you good day.' And Fox turned and, insolently, marched off.

He rounded the small promontory which opened up a view of the little bay with the launch all ready to go, men at the oars and the sails set and shivering. He wanted to laugh and chuckle, to run and

38

caper as he had on the Thames marshes. Instead he slogged on sturdily.

A small form leaped out from a bush and began a mad run inland. Like a terrier after a rat Harrison pounced. The burly gunner scooped up the man and hefted him towards Sullivan who cocked his billy over the fair wavy hair.

The lad—he was scarcely more than nineteen—looked up with an appealing face. He saw the billy and he winced back, all the fear of the press a frightful miasma of terror in his mind.

'Belay that, Mr Sullivan! He won't give any trouble.'

They snatched the lad up and another slight form darted into view over the crest and ran breathlessly up to Fox. He saw the girl; young, pretty with the country health of flushed cheeks and red lips and sparkling eyes. Her black shawl had blown back to reveal young breasts half-hidden in the bodice of her grey dress.

'Please!' she was crying, her hands held up imploringly. 'Don't take my Tommy! Please let him go, sir. He's too young—' She caught at Fox's hand. 'Here's his certificate, sir—he forgot it this morning —we ain't had no press here for—'

But Fox could not allow himself to hear any more. He turned a face of stone to the girl. 'Any man without a certificate of exemption is liable to serve in the Navy,' he said harshly. He walked on so that the girl had to struggle to keep up. 'Please do not interfere.'

'But my Tommy—his old mother's an invalid—if he's taken what are we to do?'

'Mr Sullivan, kindly escort this lady ashore!' Fox found an infuriating absurdity in his choice of words. He added for Sullivan's benefit: 'Handsomely, mind!'

'Aye, aye, sir.' Sullivan took the girl away, half-carrying her shrieking and screaming and arm-waving figure. She knew well enough that she might not see her Tommy for years, might never see him again. No wonder the press gang had so unsavoury a reputation. No wonder they sang songs in which the press figured as the embodiment of evil, and broadsheets carried pictures of debased animals dressed in sailor clothes carrying off poor innocents. It was all true, God help him, all true.

Still concerned over the boat from *Thunderer*, Fox steered the launch well out into the offing. The boat was still beached and there was no sign of Cathcart or his men. Fox permitted himself a flicker of a smile. Cathcart would find little pickings ashore after Fox had aroused the countryside with his night's depredations.

Now, thrashing along with the westerly, he was able to take stock of what he had accomplished. There were sixteen landsmen being as sick as dogs. And there were twenty-one fishermen, and of them he'd stake a great deal that the majority were prime seamen. The giant, for instance, had a thin gold ring in one ear, and if that wasn't an indication of a seaman then Fox didn't know what was. All in all, a good night's work. He just did not think about the certificates of exemption. His warrant officers had reported to him that the men taken up by the press had no certificates. Therefore—they did not have them. Fox stubbornly refused to think of the retribution in store. A commission as confused with special orders as *Duchess*'s would throw up many strange situations. They might even receive orders to sail around the Horn and enter the Pacific, although that was almost as unlikely as being ordered to sail for the Moon.

The men when they glanced aft at the erect and rigid figure of Lieutenant Fox sitting in the stern-sheets could never guess at his tormented thoughts. He was only too well aware that he was the most hated man aboard, probably one of the most hated officers in the entire Royal Navy. Had he been a man given to emotional outbursts he would have cocked his chin higher at the thought and arrogantly spat contempt on all the world. The press would always bring up bitter and agonising memories of his young brother Alfred. Alfred, so gay and lighthearted, of the sweet nature and sturdy loyalty, penned in a body fate had in some cruel way seen fit to make less than strong enough to contain so rare a spirit, Alfred, and the press were inseparably linked in Fox's mind.

With his poverty-stricken background as an urchin skyving around the Rotherhithe dockyards, fowling on the Thames marshes, rowing boats whenever he could, playing pranks on anything with a scrap of gold lace on its hat, was it any wonder that his manners and airs and graces were fathoms removed from those of the quarterdeck and so much more akin to the lower deck? Was it any wonder that he had to remove himself to some cultural limbo where he could obtain obedience from one and professional respect from the other?

He tacked the launch with a nonchalant skill he was scarcely aware of; he could sail a boat in any weather and play a hand of *vingt-et-un* on the stern-sheets. He crisped out his orders as they hooked on to *Duchess*'s main chains. First out of the launch, he touched his cap to the quarterdeck and then went at once to report to the captain.

From the aft cabin skylight voices lifted. He had taken this route deliberately to avoid Beckworth; but now the voice of the first lieutenant rose on a pitch of incredulity. The other voices were those of Struthers and the new midshipman, Haines.

'Scum, you mean, my dear Ashley? I can scarcely believe it, it so exactly confirms my own impression of the fellow.'

Now Struthers' rumble interrupted. 'He is a sound seaman and a fine officer, Mr Haines. What you say may be true—I do not, of course, doubt your word for an instant—but Mr Fox is known to me as the officer who was first aboard *Nuestro Señora del Salvator.*' At this Fox touched his finger tips to the sword at his side. He listened with a face in which not a muscle moved. The Patriotic fund had voted his first lieutenant in that action a sword to the value of fifty guineas—Fox had quite illegally taken a sword from one of the Dons he had cut down with a common cutlass.

42

'I feel we ought to try to get him out of the ship,' said Beckworth. 'I mean, there are limits to which a gentleman can go—rubbing shoulders with riff-raff like that—what would my father say?'

This time Struthers' voice came quickly and a trifle sharply.

'Any decisions regarding the officering of my ship, Mr Beckworth, will be taken by me. You are aware of that. Now, I suggest you leave off this subject. Mr Haines, you will rapidly acquaint yourself with your duties aboard. You will find a frigate is very different from a line of battle ship.'

'Of course, sir.' Haines' voice contained no trace of apology. 'I just thought you would like to know. I felt it my duty to find out what I could of the officers among whom I was to serve.'

'Quite so.'

Fox had stood enough of this. He felt no whit of shame at his common antecedents—he'd give fifty of these titled incompetents for just one horny-handed Thames lighterman—but he resented being put down merely because of an accident of birth. He clumped his feet on the companionway and clattered down towards the marine sentry. That man, as ever wooden-faced, took one look at Fox's face and wished himself safely around the lower deck mainmast once more.

The atmosphere in the aft cabin felt strained to Fox. They had just been speaking of him—and here he was. He reported in his catch—sixteen landsmen and twenty-one seamen or probable seamen. Haines, with a sidelong look at Fox, departed. Struthers rubbed his hands and beamed.

'You've done well, Mr Fox. I shall not forget it. Mr Beckworth has brought ten from the guardship, and we've had another ten Quota Men—'

'Scum, riff-raff, useless,' put in Beckworth.

'Quite so. But they can be put to the capstan and the pumps, they can run and fetch and carry. And—'

'And,' finished Fox. 'they are bodies that may take the shot intended for more valuable men.'

'Quite—ah hum—so,' said Struthers.

With fifty-seven extra men *Duchess* could sail with a little more confidence. The shot holes had been repaired; fresh water and some few fresh provisions had been brought aboard (she had been at sea for only a short time in any case) and with the mysterious passenger due at any moment the ship began to take up that rhythm peculiar to a King's ship in time of war.

The passenger came aboard just before the turn of tide and went directly below and to the captain's cabin. Fox caught a glimpse of a figure wrapped in a boat cloak and wearing an odd-looking cocked hat before it vanished from his view.

Fox thought how nice it would be to order Mr Midshipman Ashley Haines to clean out the heads for three months.

As was usual he took the ship out. Beckworth, it is true, stood on the quarterdeck with the captain; but they passed their orders through Fox, who amended them as he saw fit. It wouldn't have done for Captain Cuthbert Rowlands. By God, it wouldn't!

The master acquiesced in the arrangement and no doubt felt a little more secure for that. The Quota Men and the human derelicts from the guardship had their first taste of naval discipline. The old hands of the crew helped in putting the correct sheets into the hands of the landsmen Fox had brought and the bosun's mates thwacked their starters down to make them go and grabbed shoulders and hair—what was left of it after the shears—to make them belay, when all the yelling of 'avast!' and 'belay' brought only bewilderment.

The topman scampered aloft and the frigate's sails dropped and were sheeted home. The wind and the tide were both favourable, and with the quartermaster himself, Mr Benfield, at the wheel *Duchess* hauled smoothly out to sea.

There was no privacy for the common man aboard a frigate. The captain's cabin offered some privacy and the first lieutenant had a cubbyhole fashioned from collapsible bulkheads. The officers messed in the wardroom. Fox stood his watch during which the traverse board was written up and he kept a vigilant watch out and exchanged less than a dozen words with the quartermaster's mate at the wheel and made sure the glasses were changed promptly, and nothing happened, and then went below when he was relieved.

Later on after visiting the heads in the wardroom he passed Beckworth's cabin bulkhead. The door was shut but light shone through the cracks. He

45

heard the low mutter of voices and recognised
Haines. A sudden and quite unexpected flutter of
pink and black surrounded the vision in his left eye
and he could feel his cheek muscles fluttering.
Standing there, silent and savage, he fought for self-
control.

He had to stand for those few minutes. He could
not move on. The shame of knowing that he was
incapable of action seared into his mind. Damn
Beckworth! Damn Haines! Then, being anything but
a gentleman, he put his still-good right eye to the
crack. He could see a tangle of blankets hanging
over Beckworth's slung hammock. A naked arm
with little hair and a naked leg with only a little
more, waved. Beckworth laughed. The hammock
heaved. White skin showed. Disgust shook Fox. He
stood back, shaking. Death lay in his hands.

Haines was saying softly: 'God but this is good,
Charley.'

Both men toppled from the hammock in a tangle
of blankets. Fox heard Beckworth curse. 'Quiet,
Ashley, for God's sake!'

Fox turned and fairly ran back into the wardroom, blundered against a twelve-pounder, hit his
head against a deck beam, tripped, found time to be
profoundly thankful that Edmunds was on watch,
and collapsed into his hammock. The feel of the
ship beneath and all around him, the thrum of rigging transmitted to the hull through the chains,
the swish and slosh of water overside, all came to
him as through a thick porridge. He lay for some
time trembling. Inevitably, memories of Mr Doherty

46

tormented him. He would say nothing. It was his word against that of two gentlemen. The death in his hands was worthless.

He tried to sleep and the next moment, it seemed, he was being awoken by the marine servant with the routine news of the morning and another day's service to fill.

Trouble was always to be expected from newly-pressed men. This bunch proved no exception. The black-haired Cornish giant, one Tregarthen, had knocked down Mr Gold, the master-at-arms, giving him a bloody nose and a black eye. Mr Gold, as the master-at-arms, the regulating officer responsible for discipline aboard ship, was naturally enraged. The affair could not be passed over as Fox would have wished. Tregarthen had made himself liable to death or such lesser punishment as the captain might choose to deal from the awesome array provided him by the Articles of War.

Anyway, an example this early would bear fruit later on. Out in the Channel with the wind from the north west, steering south on the starboard tack, *Duchess* was readied. The pipes twittered 'hands to witness punishment'. Tregarthen was stripped and lashed to the gratings. The marines stood in a scarlet line across the deck. The drums rolled. Fox stood by, watching with only a part of his attention. Flogging was the accepted means by which discipline was maintained. That was the King's Regulations. Had there been other more effective ways, Fox would have welcomed them. Barrel punishments, and running the gauntlet, all those sort of fancy ideas, were no doubt excellent. But the men had to see the lash go whistling down, see the blood spurt and the flesh hang in ribbons, hear the shrieks of the victim as he gobbled out his bite of wood, for them to understand fully the rewards they would receive for the slightest indiscipline.

A flogging around the fleet meant, to Fox, the waste of a good man. A straightforward flogging like this—and he'd seen hundreds in his time—was a mere part and parcel of ship routine. Authority had to be maintained.

When it was over and Tregarthen had been dragged off the hands were piped down and Fox could get on with the real business of running a ship of war. A ship's boy darted up with the request that he speak with the captain at once.

Struthers, in his aft cabin, sat watchfully. Beckworth stood, bent beneath the beams, eyeing the passenger with all the curiosity of a cat at a mousehole.

The passenger was a young man, possessed of a quick alert face. He was dressed as a civilian, which did not make Fox's mind, as he entered, any the easier.

'This is my second lieutenant, Mr Fox,' Struthers said. He got his mouth around the words as though eating hot porridge.

Fox inclined his head just enough to indicate his acknowledgement and waited for the passenger to be introduced in turn; the captain set great store by these empty formalities.

Instead, Struthers went briskly on: 'Mr Fox, I have to inform you that it will be your duty to place this gentleman safely on shore in France at a spot I shall acquaint you with at a later date.'

CHAPTER FOUR

A spy.

They were landing a spy on the coast of France.

Well—Fox strained his eyes through the darkness seeking for the loom of Saint Etienne's point—it made a change and any change was welcome from blockade duty.

The sharpest-eyed men were posted in the tops as lookouts. Not a light showed aboard *Duchess*. She crept along under triple-reefed topsails and a single jib, her driver taut and under immediate control by a gang of skilled seamen awaiting instantaneous action in response to Fox's whispered commands. Beckworth stood by the quarterdeck rail and Edmunds was in the eyes of the ship; the captain and the passenger paced the weather side of the quarterdeck, a constant irritation to Fox.

The wind was three points abaft their starboard quarter but it was fitful and like to die away altogether soon. The triple reefs might be totally unnecessary. In the chains the leadsman continually sounded but instead of singing out his soundings were reported back by a chain of men whispering to each other fiercely through the darkness. Fox didn't like it; but Struthers accepted his judgment of the situation.

A relay man hanging to the starboard main shrouds leaned over and his words came far too loudly to Fox on the quarterdeck aft and below.

'Land dead ahead, sir!'

At once Fox gave the orders the men had been waiting for and *Duchess* rounded to and glided to a halt as silent as the bringing in of all sail could ever be silent. She rocked on the swell. It was up to Sullivan, now, to manage the tricky business of swinging out the cutter. Struthers wasn't going to risk the rattling roar of letting go the anchor.

When the cutter was in the water, Fox, Mr Midshipman Haines, who had, surprisingly enough to Fox in view of his gentlemanly scruples, not seemed to mind being detailed, and the passenger scrambled aboard. Everything loomed massy and ghostly in the darkness. The moon would be later still tonight even than it had when Fox had gone man-hunting. With muffled oars the boat's crew gave way and, with the captain's coxswain, Lampitt, muttering threats to the first man who caught a crab, the cutter pushed off into the darkness.

Among the oarsmen Fox had seen the young fair-haired boy he had snatched from the arms of his sweetheart. As a fisherman he was used to rowing and *Duchess* needed every man to pull his weight now.

Fox took the tiller himself, just as he'd made damn sure he'd been the last man into the boat.

They pulled silently through the gloom. *Duchess* vanished behind them almost at once and Fox with his free hand kept the compass constantly in view. All ahead of them beyond the muddy banks of the Laronne the land lay a tangled mess of swamps and marshes and muddy inlets. On the few high roads raised on dikes, the armed soldiers of the French Republic would be watching and waiting for just such desperate enterprises as this.

No doubt there would be forts. The charts showed that on this mouth if they lay well across to the north they could slip past the main fort on the south bank. The spy must be given a chance of life. If they landed him too far away from habitation he'd be picked up at the first crack of dawn. The French patrols were experts at rounding up dissident Royalists and Girondins and an English spy would give them the same pleasure.

'Keep the lead going there,' ordered Fox, his voice hoarse. Steadily the oars pulled and feathered, sending the boat gliding through the inky darkness. An abrupt hail reached them across the water. The boat glided on. Again the French voice lifted in the night.

A livid orange flash split the blackness. Somewhere sounded the fall of the ball. The first shot, obviously fired at random, was followed immediately by eight or nine more. Water churned around the boat. Fox did not hesitate. He could order the men to lay on their oars and ghost in the silence, hope

53

to escape detection. But the night was slipping away. The French did not know where they were; perhaps some phosphorescence in the water, or the small sounds they must make as they rowed, had betrayed them.

'Pull, you lubbers!' he said. He urged them with an upraised fist. The compass lay at his side and from time to time he consulted it, laying off the courses in his head with automatic professionalism.

A confusion arose in the bows. The leadsman's voice had fallen silent. Fox thrust the tiller at Midshipman Haines.

'Keep her on course,' he growled and dived forward.

Someone was hit and groaning. He saw a confused tangle of bodies. A splash sounded overside. In the water he saw the upraised arms and the white agonised face of young Tommy. The boy was shouting for help. His voice carried.

Again Fox did not hesitate. He should have. Even as he took off in a shallow dive into the water he knew he was doing the wrong thing. But —he could not explain it—he remembered that young girl, and the way her immature breasts had heaved so beneath the thin bodice, the way her eyes had appealed to him, her upraised arms, just like the upraised arms of Tommy in the water before him now.

He grabbed the boy, hit him alongside the jaw, began to swim back. A hullaboloo had begun on the bank. Torches flared ruddily and trails of fire stretched across the water. And now the cutter was turning. He could hear men shouting aboard. He heard Haines yelling. Oars flailed.

He thrashed up to the boat and grabbed at the transom, hoisted Tommy's body up.

'Take him, cox'n.'

With a single muscular heave which threatened to rip his threadbare coat he hauled himself over the stern counter. Now the bank was alive with shouts and flares and the clatter of musketry.

The passenger turned impassively to Fox, who flopped on the sternsheets, dripping and furious.

'I think it would be best if we returned to the ship, lieutenant. There is no chance of a landing now.'

Shaking with fury, Fox gave the orders and the boat's head turned seawards. He would not speak to Haines. That sprightly midshipman had panicked. Granted Fox should have left young Tommy to drown; Haines should have kept his head.

The whole business was a mess.

Lieutenant Beckworth told him that the moment he stepped aboard the frigate.

'You incompetent lubber!' Beckworth raged. 'The whole night wasted! The operation ruined! All for the sake of a useless lubber. You should have left him, Mr Fox, indeed you should. The captain will have something to say to you, believe me!'

Fox could only agree, silently. He had made a complete foul up of it all. Haines had only compounded the mischief.

Nothing—but nothing—must be allowed to

come between an officer of the Royal Navy and his duty.

'I expected better of you than this, Mr Fox,' Captain Struthers said, more in anger than sorrow.

All Fox's vaunted professionalism had failed him. He had imperilled an important service for the Navy by concern over the life of a young pressed man. Now they must hang about in the offing for a couple of days until the alarms on the enemy shore had died down, and then try again at their second appointed landing spot. Fox felt the weight of authority pressing him down, suffocating him; and he felt, too, the keen bite of his own conduct shaming him.

Routine followed its hallowed precedents aboard the frigate. On the second day, beating up and down, they espied the white scraps of sail over the horizon that told them they must make themselves scarce. The lookout—an old hand—reported down that he could see royals, top-gallants and topsails of the distant frigate before they dropped them below the sea rim.

'Royals!' said Beckworth, airing his knowledge for the benefit of the passenger who leaned against the rail, staring moodily out over the sea towards France. 'Froggy, by God!'

All Fox's instincts, drilled and honed by years of Naval impetuosity, drove him to bear up for that distant sail instantly and engage. But this business of spy-dropping precluded that. The passenger caught his eye. They were for a moment alone together.

'I understand your regret that you are not allowed to burn, sink and destroy that ship,' said the passenger. His light voice held a lurking humour almost lost on Fox in his present mood. 'I offer you my regrets that I so inconvenience you in your thirst for glory.'

'To hell with glory,' said George Abercrombie Fox. 'I'm after prize money.'

The passenger's eyebrows rose.

Fox had to say it. He took a grip on himself, and, harshly, said: 'I apologise for not landing you properly before, Mr—ah—Mr—?'

The spy's alert face with the hazel-coloured eyes and the thin nose and gash of mouth turned away from Fox. When he faced back again he seemed to have reached some decision.

'You may call me Roland.' He pronounced the name in the French fashion, with a nasal blast on the last syllable. 'I am not blind. I have seen aboard this ship things that astound me. You are George Abercrombie Fox, yes? Are you, by any chance, related to General Abercromby?'

Fox might have laughed, had he been a man given to empty laughter. 'No,' he said. 'I have the honour to be named for my Uncle Abercrombie. He achieved undying fame by being hanged at Tyburn.'

The mobile eyebrows lifted higher.

'Indeed!'

Fox possessed an insatiable thirst for information. He wanted to ask this man just why he was a spy, why he would risk his life ferretting about in a country whose soldiers and secret police would rejoice in parting his head from his body. The man must possess ideals, a strength of patriotism, a loyalty to a corrupt king and court in exile, perhaps—a thing Fox could more readily believe— the desire to regain lands and money and titles stolen from him by the Revolutionaries.

Then Fox was called away to deal with a routine ship matter and the chance for any more intimate tête-à-tête with spy Roland vanished. Fox had a powerful memory. He was able to remember much and store it away and draw it forth when necessary; his command of French and Spanish was complete and fluent, and, with the same gift of mimicry he could ape the fancy ways of speech of his betters. That he chose habitually to speak in a rough seaman's speech as he gave orders did nothing to endear him to crew or officers. He did not parade his gifts as he did not parade the handicap of his eye. The single item most worrying to him after the necessary provision of every last farthing to his mother and brothers and sisters ashore, and after his desire to gain promotion, was the disturbing fullness of his waistline. Aboard a King's ship with the food available he was never likely to grow fat; but ashore with eating to gluttony as was the common practice of the time, his weight problem would have been acute. He was no lean tall handsome man of a maiden's dream.

Two nights later *Duchess* ran in and they tried again.

That day the giant Cornishman had revealed a little more of his brutish character. Recovered from his flogging he had been violent with some of the other pressed men, threatening to kill the officers, threatening that he would never serve again. He was a trained seaman, who could hand, reef and steer, as the phrase had it, but his value was now problematical. A ship's boy had been found badly beaten and unable to vouchsafe an explanation of his condition. Fox suspected that the giant, Tregarthen, had been responsible, venting his unsatisfied vengeance on a lad; but there was no proof.

If there was a weakness in Fox's character it was that he felt far too kindly disposed towards ship's boys. He hated to see them abused. Strongly heterosexual himself, he felt bilious nausea at ill-treatment of ship's boys. The powder monkeys had a life far too savage and cruel as it was in the ordinary course of things for any further outrages to be heaped on them. Some of that feeling had caused him to rescue young Tommy and thus imperil the service on which *Duchess* was engaged. He knew that he could not alter that part of himself now. Injustice he resented when he would not blink an eye at a hundred lashes bestowed on a malefactor.

When the launch was readied under the intolerant eye of Sullivan himself, Fox was down in the captain's cabin studying the charts yet again.

'I shall not venture in so far tonight, Mr Fox, and as you are entering a wider mouth of the Laronne you can sail up for a good way.' Struthers spoke with his habitual authority. It wasn't that as a captain he was incompetent, so Fox thought resentfully, it was just that he did not use his reasoning powers; he was brave and capable but stupid. However, this reasoning seemed good. Fox nodded agreement.

There was a strong fort sited on the point which probably mounted forty-two pounders. If *Duchess* fell to leeward there the fort would blow her out of the water.

Tonight he was taking Midshipman Lunt. The boy had got over his shock at the death of Milne and he was as useful as a middy should be, far preferable to the nincompoop Haines. When the cox'n, the passenger and Lunt were in the launch, Fox swung down into her and took the tiller.

'Give way,' he ordered harshly. As soon as they were clear of the ship he had the masts raised and sail set and they glided in smoothly enough towards the dark and confused mass of the shore. There was more light tonight with the absence of cloud. The launch sailed into the mouth of the river well away from the French fort and Fox began to think things would go well. At this distance from England a frigate had been required for the job which, closer to home, would have been done by a lugger or cutter.

Struthers had been close-mouthed about the fullness of his orders. Fox kept in his mind the knowledge that they had seen the royals and topgallants of a French frigate. By dawn tomorrow they might

60

have to fight their way out. Then a cutter—even a sloop—would be useless against a frigate.

That brought up unpleasant memories of Struthers' ineffectual action with the French lugger. Fox put that out of his mind and concentrated on his navigation. The sails came down and the men bent to the oars. The bank drifted past, a sombre mass against starshine on the water. The spy, Roland, touched him on the shoulder.

'There, I think, Mr Fox.'

He pointed to where a frazzly clump of trees hung over the water. They must be far enough up now for the spy to be able to land and reach far enough inland before morning to be clear of the coast patrols. Time was ticking by.

The boat's stem touched mud and she swung into the shore. No one spoke. Roland stood up as the boat rocked and stepped overside. Mud made a soft sucking sound. He turned back, his face white in the starshine, and reached out a hand.

'My sincerest thanks, Mr. Fox. You—'

Fox stilled him with a fiercely whispered curse.

A horseman rode slowly out from the clump of trees. He wore a bicorne and the slanting barrel of his carbine showed a steely glitter. He had not seen them.

The slightest sound would betray them. A single shot, a shout, and the bank would swarm with men as it had on the previous night. But now they were far more exposed, far more vulnerable. Fox felt the iciness of the situation reaching him.

Lunt half lifted a hand. He held a pistol.

'Put that down!' Fox spoke the words soundlessly, forming his lips to them, as he pressed the pistol down.

Roland stood on the bank, his hand still foolishly outstretched. On his face the look of pent-up anger and frustration triggered Fox's reactions.

Fox took out that neatly-folded black kerchief. He shook it out, triangled it, gripped the two ends. He fumbled out a pistol ball, lodged it securely in the fold of cloth and then calculatingly measured the distance as he had so often done on the Thames marshes. This time he must not miss; this time more than a wildfowl supper depended on his aim.

He stood up, balanced to the rock of the boat, whirled the sling. The ball flew true. The horseman collapsed without a sound and fell from his horse.

Roland showed a face split by a delighted smile, then he was scrambling up the bank and vanishing into the darkness.

'Push off!' said Fox, in a hoarse and abusive way.

In silent obedience the bowman thrust his boat-hook.

With only the faintest tinkling of water the launch moved into midstream. As the oarsmen settled to their rhythm, young Lunt turned to Fox. His eyes were wide open and he breathed a little too unsteadily for Fox's liking.

'That was magnificent, sir!'

'Stow your bag, Mr Lunt.' Fox snarled an order at the boat's crew. 'Keep your eyes inboard there, and not a sound or I'll have the hide off to your backbones!'

62

All he'd done was to knock a stupid sentry off his horse with a slingshot. This wide-eyed middy seemed to think he'd won a major naval action; if Fox hadn't known better he'd have thought that was hero-worship shining in the boy's eyes. There was a lot more to life than simply carrying out one's orders. A damn sight more.

No one in this man's Navy, Fox knew so bitterly well, could ever regard him with genuine liking.

Lunt relapsed into silence, as he had been ordered; but the lift of his shoulder pointed at Fox indicated a hurt and smarting young man.

The need for silence was still as imperative as ever if spy Roland was to have a chance. Fox brooded. If anything, the sky was lightening, although that could be a trick of heightened nerves. In an almost complete silence the boat retraced its course. Darkness shrouded the estuary mouth but Fox did not entertain the slightest doubt about his navigation. He did not think about it. If *Duchess* was where he'd left her, then he'd come smack up to her, wind and tide and all the other factors calculated out in his head adding up to a reckoning.

At first Fox wasn't absolutely sure that what his ears told him he was hearing was a fact. Even so he reacted to what the sounds of distant shouting, a pistol shot, a confused hammering, must mean before either Lunt or Lampitt.

'Easy on your oars,' he growled. He peered ahead. Faintly, like a disembodied collection of ghostly arms, he could make out the darker shape of

Duchess in the water. The noise from her was now unmistakable.

Fox stood up in the sternsheets moving with unthinking grace to the motion of the boat. He drew his pistol and cocked it with one hard thumb.

'If any man makes a sound I'll pistol him where he sits!'

The men stared back at him, their faces blank or amazed, dumbfounded or furious, and their mouths, eyes and ears wide open.

'Give way—handsomely!' He sat down but kept himself erect, his right hand and elbow loosely grasping the tiller, his left holding that menacing pistol on his boat's crew. 'This is no time to mutiny! Not here, on Monsieur Crapaud's back door step! I'm going to put down that nonsense aboard, and you men will do your duty and stand by me!'

Now the shrieks and yells, the pistol and musket shots, aboard *Duchess,* where red roaring mutiny exploded to leave bodies rolling in the scuppers and the white decks stained with blood, rose to a crescendo of noise. Bedlam raged across the decks. But the noise boomed aft. The mutineers were winning. Fox could see the flash of muskets from the quarter deck rail—then they vanished. The marines had been swept aside. *Duchess* was firmly in the hands of mutineers.

CHAPTER FIVE

George Abercrombie Fox could see perfectly clearly as the launch hooked on to the fore chains and swung in to *Duchess*'s larboard bow beneath the curved flukes of the anchor and the arrogant jut of the cathead. Fox went up hand over hand on to the forecastle. He wondered once—and then forgot —how long his eyesight would remain good.

Lunt followed him, with Lampitt remaining to make sure the men followed. Fox had to trust them. He had to stake his faith in Naval discipline and his own stamp of authority on that belief. There was nothing else to do.

Most of the noise and confusion aft had ceased. He could hear men's voices raised in anger, shouts and catcalls and every now and then a single pistol shot. The crew must have swept the decks and penned the officers and the loyal hands aft. If only Struthers—supposing him to be still alive—seized the opportunity Fox was about to make they could take the mutineers and squeeze them as you squeezed a lime in the tropics.

Fox drew his pistol again and ran down the larboard gangway. He had to jump over the bodies scattered here and there. Abaft the mainmast a whole clump of men lay and in the starlight glitter the streams of blood looked like rivers of black ink. He went on at a rush.

Lights showed now as lanterns were brought. He guessed they were so that marksmen in the crew could pick off the officers. He grunted. Did the fools think they were at Spithead, or the Nore? Didn't they know they were within sight of a hostile shore? Perhaps that was their idea; they would seize the ship and hand her over to the French.

He could see the white shirts and frocks of seamen before him now, all with their backs to him. One or two were ramming down muskets, some waved cutlasses aimlessly. A pistol blammed from the quarterdeck and the ball gouged splinters from the mainmast. There were more bodies piled at the break of the deck, and a whole heap at the foot of the starboard companion. He hesitated in his rush and heard the slap of footfalls behind him. Lunt was with him. If the boat's crew wavered now, if they decided to join the mutineers, then George Abercrombie Fox's career in the Navy was finished. . . .

A voice bellowed.

'Give yourselves up, you officer bastards! Or we'll hang you yard-arm high!'

He recognised that voice. Tregarthen's voice, that

66

was. Fox searched wildly through the lantern-lit darkness for the hulking Cornishman. If his left eye went bad on him now. . . .

He had hesitated too long. . . . All the advantage of surprise was slipping away. . . . Where was Tregarthen?

Again the bull voice bellowed.

'We'll roll a barrel of powder down! Ar! We'll gi' you floggin' honest men!'

There! The giant was standing with his head thrown back, a cutless in his fist, highlighted in the gleam of a lantern. His dark tousled hair shone in the light. At that instant, as Fox spotted the ringleader, a voice lifted.

'Foxy! Look lively, mates! It's Foxy come back!'

Fox lifted his pistol and shot Tregarthen through the head. Any compunction he felt he had to quell. Instantly he leaped forward, drawing his sword, yelling.

Lunt fired, another mutineer shrieked and fell back, then Fox was laying about him, swearing at the top of his voice, berating the men, calling them all the filthy names he could think of. Then, thankfully, he heard his boat's crew rushing aft and joining in.

He ran through a cutlass-waving idiot, slashed the nose from the face of one of the landsmen he remembered had tried to resist Sullivan's cudgel. He was yelling and raving, his bloodied sword a blur. He was no fine fancy fencer; he preferred a cutlass when it came to work like this. A cutlass or a half-pike, perhaps the most deadly weapon ever invented for boarding. Small swords and rapiers or foils—they were gentleman's weapons, and Fox was no gentleman, thank God.

The afterguard made a dash. He saw Sullivan and Harrison laying about them. Lieutenant Edmunds staggered up with a broken sword looking frantic. Fox pushed him out of the way, cut down on the head of a man about to degut Lunt with his pike, kicked another in the groin. The fight raged fiercely for another few minutes; then as more men, seeing how the affair was going, threw down their arms or suddenly switched sides back to the officers, the mutiny abruptly petered out.

Fox did not disabuse himself of the idea that it was only Tregarthen's sudden death that had been the salutary cause of the mutiny's collapse. That man had aroused his faction and a small body of men, resolutely led, could achieve miracles over much larger bodies without a lead or a purpose save preserving their own lives.

The marines panted up with a sergeant in command. That meant their new officer was dead. *Duchess* was proving hard on marine officers.

He yanked Edmunds back, out of the mess.

'Where's the captain?'

Edmunds was distraught. 'Badly wounded! He was knocked on the head—that was the signal!'

Fox cursed and shoved Edmunds away, leaped for the aft cabin. More men clustered here, unable to get away, penned by a ring of pikes held in the loyal men's hands.

The slightest spark would set them off again. A

single injudicious word would remind them of what little they had to lose, how much to gain. Fox charged straight through.

'The Frogs will be tumbling out of their beds now!' he yelled. 'They'll be untangling themselves from their mademoiselles' legs! And then they'll be blaming us!'

Someone laughed. He felt the air of tension subtly change. Men were like sheep.

'Get to your quarters. We'll be in action soon. I'll expect every mother's son of you to fight like you've never fought before! Mr Sullivan! Mr Harrison!' He would have called for the master-at-arms; but he had a shrewd suspicion that that unfortunate would be the first to be murdered in any mutiny. 'I want the ship spick-and-span! Bristol fashion! Get the decks scrubbed——' He yelled a whole volley of orders, anything, to get the men back into the frame of mind the Navy demanded before an action.

As though Heaven was at last condescending to him a rocket flashed a trail of golden fire across the sky.

'There!' he pointed dramatically. 'That's where your enemy is! Every blagskite of you is going to fight or I'll know the reason why!'

Now the loyal men outnumbered the quondam mutineers. The marines held their muskets at the present. The moment hung.

Then someone let out a yell. 'Old Foxey may be the blackest bastard in the Navy—but if he says so —it is!'

A roar greeted this. The men surged forward.

Fox whispered a vicious order to his warrant officers.

'No rattans or rope's-ends, mind! They'll not take it, not in their frame of mind.'

'Aye, aye, sir,' said Sullivan. He had a gash over his forehead; but he appeared to be otherwise unharmed.

Edmunds stumbled up, his face ghastly.

Edmunds was simply a naval officer like Fox, without prospects or influence and because of that, certainly not because he felt any sympathy or liking for him, Fox felt he must snap Edmunds' mind back into accustomed grooves.

'Mr Edmunds!' he said in the most unpleasant tone he was capable of. 'I want the ship under way at once. Weigh anchor and set all plain sail if you please!'

The immediate response, uttered by Edmunds before he quite realised, 'Aye, aye, sir,' cheered Fox.

'The course will be west by north.'

'Aye, aye, sir,' said Edmunds again; but this time the words were fuller, more assured. Edmunds went about the business of making sail and weighing anchor as Fox pushed through the powder-burned aft cabin door. The cabin was empty. He looked about and then heard a murmur of voices beneath his feet. The smile that almost widened his lips was scornful, contemptuous, unpleasant.

He bashed his pistol butt on the deck.

'You can come out now,' he bawled. Then, after what he felt was an insolently long-enough lapse of time, he added: 'Sir.'

Getting the men hiding in the cramped space above the rudder out was simple enough except for Captain Struthers. He was in a bad way, raving, delirious, with a crack on his head that should have killed him. His steward kept trying to swab the blood away. The purser was there, his fat cheeks shrunken. Mr Midshipman Haines looked as though he had not only vomited over his fancy white waistcoat but had fouled his breeches. Lieutenant Beckworth, his handsome face fine-drawn, his nostrils quivering, peered about suspiciously. Fox guessed what the man was thinking and he had to restrain himself from knocking Beckworth down.

'It's all clear now, sir,' he said formally. 'The men are back to their duty.'

'The ship's moving!'

'Yes, sir, I felt it best, in the absence of the captain, to move ourselves from under the French guns.'

'You'd no damn business sailing the ship without orders!'

Fox had heard all this before.

'There have been a considerable number of casualties.' He checked as the master, Mr Showell, crawled out. He could not blame that white-haired man for hiding. 'Mr Showell, would you be good enough to attend to the wheel—Mr Edmunds has the deck. We steer west by north.'

The situation had relapsed into its cynical pattern so fast Fox gratified himself by his own amusement. Beckworth said: 'Belay that, Mr Showell. West by north? That'll take us into the shoals—steer north west by north, Mr Showell, if you please.'

'Aye, aye, sir,' said the master, his old face tired. He went out. Fox kept his seething anger down.

'I should like to point out, sir, that the new course will carry us close to the fort—that's *Fort du Peuple*, sir—'

'I am aware, Mr Fox, that you are often allowed to regulate the conduct of this ship. But at the moment Captain Struthers is incapacitated and as a consequence I am now in command. Do I make myself clear?'

You couldn't argue with that, not in the Royal Navy. The only argument had been tried a half hour before, and that had failed in blood.

Fox made himself nod—he'd lost his hat somewhere—and went back on deck. There was a very great deal to do. The doing of it occupied his mind and hands. The dead had to be laid out ready for sewing into their hammocks wedded to a twelve-pound ball, the blood must be scrubbed from the decks, the marines must be kept awake and on their toes, although Fox suspected that—at least for the moment—mutiny was dead. Once again he felt a tide of thankfulness that he'd had Lampitt, the captain's coxswain, and a loyal crew. It was only their support that had turned the tide. By himself he could have done nothing.

Mr Lunt, too, had come through with flying colours.

He studied the loom of the land off their starboard bow. *Fort du Peuple* frowned down from

72

those heights. They might slip past, it was the kind of gamble he would have taken on his own behalf; perhaps Beckworth was right. There was nothing he could do about it if Beckworth was wrong.

Then the very fact that he could faintly discern the point on which the fort had been built alarmed him. It was growing lighter. Dawn. And not a sign of a comforting sea mist, no dawn mist to cloak them as they ran the gauntlet.

He was chilled, hungry, stiff—although he scarcely noticed these minor discomforts. They had been a part of his life ever since he could remember anything. What concerned him most was the threat of those forty-two-pounders secure behind their embrasures and battlements.

Beckworth came on deck. He made no comment on the labours of the hands, on what had been achieved. He would recall only that there had been a mutiny. He would demand hangings and floggings when they reached Plymouth. He looked at the loom of the land, took a turn about the weather side of the quarterdeck, then told the quartermaster to come to north west true.

As was his wont Fox interpreted and roared out for the boatswain's mates to call the hands on watch to swing the yards. The familiar sounds soothed him. If the wind held steady they could weather the point easily—a much easier piece of straightforward sailing than his desire to sail close-hauled nearer the rocks and shoals of the south-western side of the estuary's mouth. Beckworth ignored the bustle. He walked as though conscious of his own dignity. Gradually the conviction stole over Fox that Beckworth really thought himself capable of captaining a King's ship. The idea appalled Fox.

Abruptly Beckworth spoke and what he said drove the last nail into Fox's hopes.

'I have been a loyal first lieutenant to Captain Struthers. I have allowed you an unprecedented leeway. But from now on you have better remember that I am in command. I will not tolerate the slightest infringement on my position, is that clear?'

'Aye, aye, sir.' Fox ground the words out. He could do no more.

'Since you have seen fit to send all hands back to stations and have not taken the trouble to confine the ringleaders below in irons, we shall have some difficulty in sorting out the sheep from the goats. But I shall do it, never fear.'

'I shot the ringleader and cut down the other fools,' said Fox.

'Oh?' Beckworth had been jolted at that.

'The men will follow any strong lead. Tregarthen aroused them—the mutineers are dead, sir. The hands will remain loyal now, I have no doubt.' He wanted to add: 'So there will be no need for retribution at Plymouth.' But he did not do so. To have done so would have been the surest way to ensure Beckworth's spite against the deluded men.

Where yesterday Fox would simply have ordered the thing himself, today, with this incompetent in command resentful of the slightest implied slur, he had to be more cautious. He said carefully: 'I do not hear the leadsman very clearly, sir.'

Beckworth bristled. He roared out: 'Leadsman! Rouse yourself! Let's hear your soundings!'

With that Fox was able to shout: 'Put the best man in the chains, there! Keep the soundings going!'

Beckworth glared at him; but the ticklish thing had been done, and done without trouble.

Mr Showell caught Fox's eye; but neither betrayed by so much as a single muscle tremor what their thoughts were.

The point was close on them now. With the brightening light hidden from them by the land mass to the east, the fort lay in shadow. Steadily *Duchess* forged on. The wind would begin to turn fluky now, recalcitrant, with the growing heat of the morning, and *Duchess* would have to be handled with split-second timing. The advantage of the ebb tide was failing fast. It was all going to be extremely tricky.

Fox kept his eyes continually sweeping the entire three hundred and sixty degrees he could cover; yet he was looking directly at the fort's hidden presence when the first blossom of white smoke broke into life, expanded and drifted away. The forty-two pound shot hissed into the sea a cable's length away to starboard.

'Short!' said Beckworth, as though he had arranged it.

The men were at their action stations now. Fox had seen to it that they had had breakfast, and that the ship was in as fit a state as possible to fight an action. The galley fires were out; the deck had been sanded; the shot garlands between the guns were full; the collapsible bulkheads had been torn down —and Captain Struthers had been removed to the orlop.

Mr Edmunds stood by the mainmast in command of the starboard battery. There had been gaps in the watchbill and Fox had had to re-arrange the orders. Mr Lunt would handle the port battery—a wild thing for a midshipman after landing a spy on the French coast and helping quell a mutiny. Fox just prayed that Beckworth would not order him from the quarterdeck; but evidently Beckworth's dreams of command included, as was usual, having his first lieutenant with him. The second puff of white blossomed. This time the shot roused a spout half a cable's length off.

'Give 'em another ten minutes,' said Mr Showell softly to Fox. 'They'll have their fires hot by then.'

Fox nodded without speaking. Any sailor man felt a damp chill up the spine at the thought of red-hot shot.

A whole row of smoke puffs bloomed from the still-hidden fort. The sea off the starboard bow and beam churned into a maelstrom of foam.

Fox cocked an eye. There had been at least fifteen shots. The range was coming down all the time. His gunner's mind ticked off angles and velocities, all the ballistic expertise that had come so easily to him originated he supposed in those boyhood days of wildfowling. He used to be fond of saying: 'If I can see it I can hit it.' But since his trouble with his eyes he'd dropped that saying. Now he just knew that, given a prior knowledge of the

76

idiosyncracies of the gun he was using, he could hit his target at reasonable range nine times out of ten. With a pistol, of course, he would never dream of missing. There was no braggadocio in this, just a plain assessment of factors on which his life could depend.

Now he reckoned that, if he laid the gun himself, he could put a shot into the fort. Not that that would make much difference, one twelve-pounder would hardly be noticed.

Once more the fort erupted in white smoke. The air was suddenly filled with an eerie moaning. He heard a sickening crash from forward. A halliard parted with a crack like a snapped whip. The men around the starboard aft carronade abruptly disintegrated into a red and sticky mess and Mr Showell staggered away, his white hair bedabbled with blood. The ship heaved up on the long low swell.

'Get that halliard spliced!' Fox roared.

Men were clearing the carronade's crew away.

Beckworth was gripping the quarterdeck rail, staring forwards and up, his face wild.

'Fire!' he screamed. 'Mr Edmunds—what are you waiting for! Fire, Goddamn you!'

Edmunds' voice shouted: 'Fire!' and the twelve twelve-pounders crashed out. Their trucks rumbled on the deck like hollow-drums, vibrating the fabric of the ship. Naked arms frantically wielded worms clearing out the fragments of spent cartridge, damp sponges thrust down smoking bores, the cartridges went thrust down and the twelve-pound balls rammed home. It was all done smartly enough; Fox felt the black thoughts of mutiny impelled those sweating guns' crews.

'Cock your locks! Fire—stop your vents!'

Again the broadside crashed out and the ship heeled.

But through the smoke an answering avalanche struck home. Fox saw a twelve-pounder rear into the air and, toppled like a child's top, cartwheel across the next gun. Men were flung screaming. A cascading gout of splinters fountained from the mainmast and men at the guns clawed as arrow-like splinters tore into them.

Then—from the waist, below the gangway, where a ball had struck home came the shout most dreaded of all.

'Fire!'

The French had stoked their fires and heated their shot. Red-hot shot had smashed into *Duchess*. Smoke wreathed evilly above the gangway.

'Fire! The ship's on fire!'

CHAPTER SIX

If anything at all was to be done to save *Duchess* it must be done *now*.

Haines was standing staring down stupidly on that evilly-rising oily smoke. His white face showed absolute terror.

'Out of my way!' yelled Fox.

He crashed along the gangway and fairly hurled himself on to the main deck. The marines lining the side remained facing overside, their muskets at their sides.

'Water!' screamed Fox. He snatched up a ready bucket and hurled its contents over the smoke. At its heart he could see the flicker of flame. A twelve-pounder had been run up, the captain of the gun standing with the lanyard in his hand, but it had not yet fired. The crew were staring at the smoke and flame.

'Belay firing!' yelled Fox. 'Get this bloody fire out! Jump to it if you don't want to be fried!'

Men suddenly broke their stasis and rushed forward; buckets of water miraculously appeared and the flames hissed and sizzled with baffled malice. Through it all another French broadside from the fort crashed home. A man beside Horner, a boatswain's mate about to hand across a bucket of water, dropped the bucket as Horner reared up. A two-foot splinter of wood had speared through his face, transfixing his cheeks, spouting blood onto the deck. He was one of the loyal men of the mutiny. Fox had no time to check his falling body. He yelled for someone to clear the man away, and dashed a fresh bucket of water onto the flames.

Only his prompt action had given them any chance. Now with buckets hurling sea water in a steady stream, the flames curled and writhed, the smoke thickened and then, when Fox had thought it too late, the fire died to leave a great mess of charred wood and a stink that tasted flat and sulphurous on the tongue.

Noise gonged in Fox's head. He was drenched with sweat and water—and, as seemed inevitable, someone's blood had splattered all across him. He wiped his sleeve over his face. Something was missing. He braced to the heave of the ship and prepared to order the men back to the guns.

Beckworth's voice licked out. 'Cease fire!'

As the smoke cleared Fox saw *Duchess* had weathered the point, had left *Fort de Peuple* behind, and could draw out to a fuller canvas and drop the coast of France astern.

In the midst of the momentary silence, a silence

of gratitude and relaxation of tension, a voice bellowed.

'Sail ho! Square on the larboard beam!' The voice screeched with excitement. 'A Frenchy! She's got Royals set—a French frigate!'

Fox felt a sudden numbing sense of crushing defeat. They had battled past the fort and lost how many men he didn't yet know doing it, they'd almost burned, and now, in the moment of success, they were caught between the shore and a French frigate who had the weather gage.

Life could seldom offer any less inviting prospects.

Then the memory of the way Beckworth had ordered the gunfire, and the militarily useless expenditure of powder and shot, whatever psychological advantages may have accrued from the noise and smoke of their own guns, came to taunt Fox. They would have to fight the French frigate now. And he'd see to it that Edmunds and Lunt made better practice this time. In matters of gunnery Fox tolerated nothing short of perfection.

The thing would have to be done with style. It was useless to think that if they'd taken the course he had proposed, close-hauled, they would have had the weather gage. Any seaman worth his salt gives up not one inch of leeway.

With a roaring foul-mouthed curse Fox hurled abuse at the men, rousing them out to clear away the mess. He saw a boatswain's mate flicking a rump with a starter and he checked his automatic response. The men would know what it was all about by now.

Back on the quarterdeck he ignored Beckworth and looked long and carefully at the enemy. She had stolen in, running easily with the wind on her larboard quarter, and now she cruised in the offing in the perfect position to cut them off whatever manoeuvre they tried. She was like a terrier at a rathole—the tired old simile might be tired, but it fitted. He could see her hull clearly now; the telescope revealed fifteen ports on the gun deck and seven on the quarterdeck. A forty gun frigate, begod. Armed above her legend. And those port lids were triced up and the guns run out. The Frenchies were showing their teeth. Those teeth would be eighteen-pounders on the gun deck, more than likely, and the chances were she carried carronades—thirty-twos—on the quarterdeck. It would be a tidy old fight.

Now it was here, Fox thirsted for the action. It had to come, and he blazed with excitement for it to begin. At his side Beckworth shared that desire for action.

'This is where I get my step,' he said, coolly. 'This is more like what I expect of a naval officer than scrapping with a god-forsaken lugger.'

Fox didn't answer. His mind ran busily over the inequality of the coming action. *Duchess* had lost a lot of men. He had baulked at the idea of hurling the long row of corpses overboard—there had been no time for a formal burial—and the hands would have seen this as another affront and a clear incitement to mutiny. Those corpses were below, neatly rolled in their hammocks. But for men killed in action a different fate awaited. Nothing must be allowed to obstruct the decks. Even as Fox watched a couple of boatswain's mates heaved poor dead Horner over the side. There were far too many dead men aboard ship and not enough living.

With every passing second the two frigates neared each other. Fox smelled the wind. He looked about him. He cocked an eye at Beckworth. Surely that Honourable nincompoop wasn't just going to run up yard arm to yard arm and slug it out? But apparently, that was just what Lieutenant Beckworth intended. It was the Navy maxim. Close for action. Fox felt the old nausea, the old anger at titled incompetents, flooding him. He suspected that *Duchess* must be down to about one hundred and forty or so men and boys. That Frenchman would be packed with men, three hundred or more. And with forty guns to thirty-two—less, with the damages *Duchess* had sustained, and with those guns and carronades of significantly heavier calibre, the Frenchman would make short work of them.

Fox fumed and fretted and cursed himself for a lily-livered coward. He kept that iron mask of constraint on his face. What had the men called him— Old Foxey? Well, he was being a damned cowardly fool now, right enough.

Still Beckworth held on.

Larboard to starboard, converging, the ships held their courses.

The scarcity of men for the guns necessitated

manning only one broadside completely; the other was stripped until it should come into action. Finding competent gun captains was enormously difficult. Since the action against *Fort du Peuple* the starboard broadside was still manned; the larboard not. Now Beckworth seemed to take this in. Fox won his private gamble as to just how long it would take Beckworth to notice.

'Mr Fox! Why are the guns' crews manning the disengaged broadside? Surely I do not have to think of everything, to give you every simple order?'

Fox put on his expression of great surprise; he feigned bewilderment well.

'I understood, sir, it was your intention to haul your wind just as we reached the Frenchman, and, passing under his counter, rake him as he went.'

'Ha—hm,' said Lieutenant Beckworth. He rallied. 'Of course, of course. I just wished to see if you still had your wits about you.'

Fox could go on, now. 'She's carrying royals. That means she'll be that bit slower in stays—I should judge—and if she wears we have her between us and the shore.'

'Quite so.'

Fox saw Midshipman Haines staring at him. Seventy-Fours, on which Haines had previously served, did not always train up a young man in frigate tactics. The evolution Fox had suggested was simple-minded to the point of imbecility; but they were the kind of schemes that worked at sea.

Duchess's bowsprit was pointed in the general direction of the Frenchman's; there was nothing in their points of sailing now. Fox said: 'You might wish me to take command of the starboard battery, sir. I've had the guns triple shotted. I don't want to waste a single shot.'

'Ah—very well, Mr Fox. I shall haul up on your signal.'

'Aye, aye, sir.' Now, thought Fox to himself as he went down to the gundeck, was that simple-mindedness on Beckworth's part, deep cunning, or was his pose as the omnipotent captain wearing a little on him?

The odds were wild enough as it was. Fox had long grown accustomed to carrying bumbling superior officers full of bravado and simple nautical skills but completely lacking the finer technical points or the scheming capacity required for the outstanding success he demanded. Hauling up under an enemy's stern and raking him—what kind of manoeuvre was that? Straight out of the copy book. As easy to see as the bracing over of the yards.

The Frenchman with her royals set and drawing was fore reaching on *Duchess*. Her captain would be alert to the first indication that the British frigate was trying to rake her. The moment *Duchess*'s bowsprit swung to larboard the French frigate would haul up, too—if she did not try a more ambitious venture—and the whole weight of her broadside could crush down the length of *Duchess*.

Fox kept that set unpleasant look on his face. Not only had he to outfox the French captain, he had to manoeuvre his own commander into the bargain.

He went forward, looking keenly about him, studying the bearing of the men, how they stood, the low-voiced remarks they made, noticing every detail of the batteries of guns and ready with a harsh and intolerant word to check the slightest slackness. He called Mr Midshipman Lunt to him. The middy's face was set and white; but he looked capable and wore a fair imitation of being unafraid. There might, Fox had to admit to himself, be something in Mr Lunt.

'We're going to smash that Frenchy, Mr Lunt,' he said briskly. 'On my order—not a second before and not a second after, mind—I want you to brace over the fore top yard and fore yard and immediately bring them back. Instantly, mark you, Mr Lunt, instantly!'

'Aye, aye, sir.' Lunt understood. The middy nodded and his face showed not the blank acceptance of orders but a lively grasp of what Fox intended.

To Mr Edmunds, commanding the battery of starboard twelve-pounders, he gave orders that caused that young officer to nod, his face expressionless as was required of a naval lieutenant in moments of crisis.

'Remember, Mr Edmunds. Not a moment before my order. The Frenchman will have men in his tops, and his poopdeck sticks up a mile into the air, so he can see what we're doing down here. I want him to have no warning.'

'Aye, aye, sir.'

There just weren't men enough aboard to hand the sheets and to man the broadsides at the same time. Not trained men, that was, and a very great deal would depend on the way the mates could drive half-understanding men to stick to their work in the midst of smoke and flame and the unnerving shriek of eighteen-pound shot flying about their heads.

The two ships were nearer now. The wind still held. The land showed grey and purple off the starboard beam and the sun set golden lances across the water and threw the shadows of the ships dancing to seaward. Calculating angles with his eye, working out vectors in his head, Fox held on. If the trick failed, Beckworth could have him court-martialled and broken. Failure was no longer tolerated in the Royal Navy. Byng remained ever present in the mind of officers going into action.

Beckworth would say that Fox had disobeyed his orders. A dismasted hulk would stand as his condemnation. Still Fox held on as the ships drew closer to each other. He looked forward to where Lunt stood with his gang of landsmen at the fore braces. Failure there would mean failure all along the line. He took a breath—and that damnable ring of purple and black crept insidiously around the vision of his left eye. He cursed, wildly, luridly, beneath his breath. As though he didn't have enough to contend with—and now—this!

He forced himself to stand rigid, unmoving, watching the shape of the French frigate as the gritty and fiery pains attacked his left eye. He blinked; but that was no good. Closer—closer— *Duchess*'s bowsprit eased up past the Frenchman's starboard quarter. He could see the men on her quarterdeck, black shapes looking over the netting, see the flash wink of steel. The long row of her eighteen-pounders grinned at him.

'Mr Lunt!' Fox roared. 'Haul your braces!'

Lunt and his boatswain's mates leaped into action, the landsmen staggered back with the braces, the fore yards began to swing over. Fox had given no orders to the helmsman. He kept all his attention screwed on to the Frenchman. If she didn't haul her wind—if she refused—if her captain was a lubber— then he saw the French frigate's yards begin to swing and her rudder kick over.

'Mr Lunt!' He bellowed the order and the landsmen were staggering and falling and tailing on to the opposite braces and hauling the yards back. 'Mr Edmunds!'

The Frenchman hauled up to windward, her stern fleering around in a bubble of disturbed water. Beckworth was screeching something about the Froggy having beaten them to it and to look out for a raking broadside—Fox shut the man's voice from his mind and roared Edmund's gun crews on as they made a mad dash from starboard to larboard. The guns, already triple-shotted and run out, were all ready. *Duchess* slid back on her former course with only the slightest tremor of her canvas to indicate the swift S-turn she had made. The bowsprit surged

88

past the enemy counter and Fox could see the gilding and the ornament and the name in elegant letters all across the stern. *Mortagne*.

'Fire as your guns bear!' he yelled. 'I'll flog every man of every crew who misses!'

The bow gun fired in a gout of smoke. As the noise blammed back Fox clearly saw a stern window of *Mortagne* battered in by the shot. The other guns went off in an increasing roaring as they bore. Chips, gilding, wood flew and spouted from the Frenchman's stern. Those twelve-pounder balls would be hurtling the length of *Mortagne* now, overturning guns, pulverising men, smashing and rending and destroying their way forward.

There was no time to think of that. Hurling orders at his men as the gun trucks rumbled on the deck he brought *Duchess* around and smashed in a second broadside. The four twenty-four-pounder carronades on the quarterdeck fired together and Fox caught a swift glimpse through the smoke of the Frenchman's quarterdeck. Men had been flung back by the blast. The deck looked as though a monstrous broom had swept across it. The hammocks rolled along the rail for protection had been split and tossed and flung like feathers. *Mortagne* had been badly hit. Now Fox stared up through the smoke. The noise around him smashed in in waves, the smoke choked him, his eyes pained; but all these things were distant and removed, a part of him that had no business interfering with his job. *Mortagne*'s masts were opening out, widening, she was swinging around and now *Duchess* would have to take the crushing broadside.

Edmunds and Lunt were hard at work urging the guncrews to fiercer exertions. Harrison and Sullivan were raging among the men; the marines were firing coolly into the smoke; powder monkeys dodged through the clutter to bring fresh cartridges up from the magazines. Fox suddenly thought of what would happen to that busy scene when *Mortagne*'s broadside smote them.

'For what we are about to receive,' he said, but softly, to himself.

Here it came.

Smoke, noise, confusion. Fox saw the cutter reduced in the twinkling of an eye to matchwood. The main top gallant yard broke free from its slings and crashed down bringing a tangled mass of confusion with it. A marine stood for a second looking stupidly at his musket which was bent up into a U-shape —the man had no left arm with which to hold it. The whickering sound of the broadside faded; Fox breathed out. The Frenchmen had fired high—as was their custom—and the main topgallant was not too serious a loss at this moment; he had no men to spare anyway.

Duchess's answering broadside smashed out and more smoke gushed out to envelop the scene in a mazy darkness through which the shafts of sunlight struck as though finding their way through the leafy arcades of a forest. The ship heeled. Desperately, peering through the smoke with one good eye, Fox sought *Mortagne*'s masts. He could see her foremast, the canvas drooping, the yards slatting. Another broadside smashed in. Mr Haines was yelling like a madman.

'Mr Fox! Mr Fox! Mr Beckworth's—' The rest was lost in the renewed thunder of *Duchess*'s broadside. The guns leaped back across the deck. The frantic actions of the men in worming out, sponging, loading and ramming home were nowhere as smart as Fox wished; this was a crew who had not been under his orders long enough to weld them ito an efficient fighting machine. But they must be kept at it.

'Keep the men at it, Mr Edmunds!' he yelled, and ran for the quarterdeck.

Haines was almost blubbering.

'Mr Beckworth—a splinter—wrist—blood—blood—'

Beckworth was not on deck. Fox felt a fierce leap of joy. Now the ship was his. Now the men would obey him as the sole authority on board. Hate him they might, loathe him, resent him, a Thames waterside rat poncing about in a cocked hat and a sword; but, by God—he'd make them fight!

'I intend to board, Mr Haines,' he said, coldly, indifferent to Haines' fears. 'Go forward with the marines.'

A splinter exploded from the smoke and whined past Haines' head. He ducked and his white face turned green.

"Stand up to it, you young whelp!" Fox said,

fiercely, joyfully. 'I might be scum, but what are you?"

For a moment Haines looked at him with eyes that held an awful agony of hate; then he ran forward.

'Mr Showell! I intend to board. Hold the deck—we'll have this fat Frenchy, never fear.'

'Aye, aye, sir!' bellowed back old Showell, his white hair suddenly illuminated by a shaft of sunlight. Smoke choked the decks; more spars had fallen, but so far the masts remained upright. How much longer they could take this punishment, Fox did not know; but his determination to board was strengthened by the sheer desperation of their plight.

He snatched up a cutlass from the arms rack; his fancy Spanish sword—a rapier, really—would be next to useless in the fierce cut and thrust of a boarding bedlam.

He could see *Mortagne* briefly through the cloud banks. The wind had almost died. All around him men were shouting and screaming, working and dying. He ran forward, collecting the marines and all the men not working the guns. On the forecastle he pushed past Haines, rigid and looking as though he was drunk, and judged his distance. The French frigate's quarter showed towering above them. It would be a big jump. He felt his right eye begin to quiver and for a moment complete darkness enveloped him.

He shook his head in a panic of pain; light sifted back; he could once more see. The bows touched, the bowsprit speared into the Frenchman's mizzen rigging. Coughing smoke, his eyes red and inflamed, brandishing his cutlass, Fox leaped.

Mortagne's boarding netting had been shredded by *Duchess*'s fire. He handed himself up, tumbled over onto the deck. Blood and corpses lay everywhere. A pistol bullet knocked his hat from his head. He charged along the deck, smashed a Frenchman over the head, felt a body beside him thrust to clear another man away, kicked a face in, used the hilt of his sword in a savage downward blow, slashed the blade across a pike-wielding figure.

It was all animation, frenetic movement, the blasting of pistol shots, the shrieks of wounded men, the heave of the deck, the drifting smoke. The French tumbled off the quarterdeck. The figure beside him resolved itself into Lunt who led a party forward, clearing out the French as ferrets clear out a rabbit warren. *Mortagne* had suffered gruesomely. Bodies lay everywhere.

The British cheered and charged again. Men who the previous night had plotted mutiny now fought with halfpike and cutlass against their country's enemies. It was one way of getting rid of their energy. Landsmen, lubbers, boys and trained seamen cleared the French from the decks, drove them below, battened them down. With his own hands Fox lowered the French ensign. Lampitt, the captain's coxswain, was there, ready to bend on the Union Flag. As it rose in the clearing smoke the men cheered again. Hats were lifted. The sun shone through.

Someone, Fox did not recognise the voice, shouted: 'Old Foxey's done it! The black bastard's done it!'

He had, too. Outgunned, outmanned, from the lee gauge, Fox had taken the enemy.

CHAPTER SEVEN

Eerily, the silence crept back. From overside they could hear the slip-slop of the waves. A wounded man was screaming; but soon his cries died away in a gurgle. Canvas slatted and the blocks rattled. The sun grew and shone refulgently to reveal the two ships floating idly on the sea, with the land a mile on their lee and the wind a mere zephyr. Smoke banks hung thickly a half mile to leeward, gradually shredding and disappearing.

A voice hailed from *Duchess*'s quarterdeck, an arrogant voice, a hectoring voice.

'What are you lubbers waiting for? I want that ship ready to sail in twenty minutes! Mr Fox, come aboard. Mr Haines will take the prize into port.'

All Fox's joy evaporated. Once more the hated voice of authority took the pleasure from his accomplishment.

'Aye, aye, sir,' he bellowed back. He took a last look around the shattered deck. They were thirty-two-pounders on the quarterdeck, begod. Nimbly he sprang up into *Duchess*'s bowsprit rigging and swarmed down to the forecastle.

He wondered, not without some spite, just what Beckworth would do now. With the depleted crews it would not be an easy task to sail both ships back to England.

He was aware in a clinical way that he was tired beyond reason. He had been actively engaged all night; but mere fatigue had no place on the inventory of a Naval officer. He halted on the forecastle and scanned the land—no untoward signs there—and then to seaward. He felt a sudden and unlovely treacherous jump of enjoyment. Out there in the offing a French corvette sailed into view. She'd have twenty or twenty-two nine-pounders; no match for *Duchess* in ordinary times. But now *Duchess* was seriously undermanned for her own management, and doubly so with a prize to consider. The situation was interesting.

He reached the quarterdeck to find Beckworth eyeing the corvette, which remained in the offing under enough canvas to keep her on the wind that had failed here by the land, and the first lieutenant was biting his lip. He had wound a blood-stained rag around his wrist. Fox kept his face expressionless at that; and for the first time realised that he himself was not wounded.

Of course, Fox considered, not without a fresh lick of that vicious spite, the corvette out there might be armed with twelves. Clearly she was contemplating the two frigates and keeping them under observation and that could only mean she was expecting reinforcements; probably a couple of fine fast forty-six-gun frigates. Then what would the Honourable Charles Beckworth do?

The sound of the wounded moaning from beneath his feet in the orlop distressed Fox. He hated the aftermath of action. He was glad to see that Sullivan, as bold and brassy as ever, had survived and was driving the men to splicing and clearing away and setting the ship to rights. He itched to join in the work. And the prize must be put into a seaworthy state; luckily no important spars had been knocked away.

A puff of wind slatted the yards and the heads of the ships moved, *Duchess*'s bowsprit chafing *Mortagne*'s mizzen shrouds.

Fox opened his mouth to yell furious orders to fend off, to back *Duchess*'s topsails, to clear the growing danger of a disaster, when he caught Beckworth's eye. His open mouth was too widely distended for what he said; but he covered that anomaly by a cough, and then said: 'What are your orders, sir?'

That felt quite pleasurable.

Beckworth said: 'Ha, hm—I think—'

At that moment Captain Struthers came onto the quarterdeck.

He cast a glance about him. He nodded at sight of the French frigate. His eye took in the boatswain at work, the men in the rigging, the gathering movement of the ships as the wind got up again.

'Very good, Mr Beckworth,' Struthers said. 'A fine piece of work. I'll trouble you to back the topsails and get us free of that ship. Who have you put aboard as prize master?'

'Thank you, sir—Mr Haines, sir—'

'Send across a couple of master's mates. Tell him with my compliments to conform exactly to my movements. We'll take the prize in, Mr Beckworth.'

Fox just stood there.

Oh, yes, the full story would come out later on. But the full story, the true story, didn't matter. Beckworth had begun the action on the quarter-deck, and now here he was on the quarterdeck again in the moment of victory. It was his, that victory, all his.

All this had happened to Fox before. He should be used to it by now. It was the Navy way.

By the time the wind had risen enough to give them seaway they had patched enough sails to enable them to haul up and sail in line ahead away from the estuary of the Laronne where the grim *Fort du Peuple* frowned down. *Duchess* led. The French corvette hovered and for a moment Fox thought she might come down on them; but common sense prevailed aboard the Frenchman and she hauled off, out of range, impotently watched them sail away.

Fox fell to wondering just how much prize money he could expect. *Mortagne* was a fine ship. She could be repaired and sold into the service; the British Royal Navy's finest frigates were French prizes.

That money, if there was more than a hundred pounds he would be lucky, would go at once to his mother. The Fox family weighed on him with cares and duty; but it was a responsibility he shouldered with a dark pride. His father in dying had left the family in his charge. His father, a simple, unlettered labourer around the docks, fair game for all the hard work and kicks and for none of the ha'pence —his father had set all store by the eldest son of the family, John, who was apprenticed as carpenter in the dockyard, who would have a good job with secure prospects, a skilled man, able to support the family.

But John had died. George Abercrombie was the second son. What prospects had a ship's boy? Only the savage resolution to fend for himself and the family had kept Fox sane and purposeful in an insane and aimless world. Now he would do anything —*anything*—for the family still held together by the mother he worshipped and for whose sake he had suffered so much. He would kill without compunction. He knew that. All that meant was that he must never be caught; for without his protection his mother and the family would be in a desperate plight. There had been thirteen children, and three had died early, a clear indication of the devotion of his parents in an age of when over sixty per cent of children died before the age of five.

Fox had had his chance with Captain Cuthbert Rowlands, and he had taken it with both hands and a young brain afire for life. Now, with gentle, gallant, unique Captain Rowlands dead and gone, Fox had only his own two hands and that scheming brain of his to stand between him and the world.

Lascelles the surgeon came on deck to report the number of dead and wounded—twenty and thirty-five. Fox gripped the rail, thinking of the blood that had gouted from poor Jonas, the way the cooper's mate had stood for a long second looking stupidly at the stump of his left arm before he fell, the screech that landsman had let out when a French halfpike had torn bloodily into his guts.

The French casualties, inevitably, would be many more. *Duchess* had fired at *Mortagne*'s hull; he had seen the results of that work when he'd boarded, the decks cumbered with the dead, the blood all frothy in the scuppers. Those first two raking broadsides had settled the issue, really. With that initial damage, the Frenchman had been beaten before they'd settled broadside to broadside and Fox had led the boarders.

Fatigue tried to drag him down; but there was far too much to do, even after such a night and a morning, and he kept himself at the work, driving himself as he drove the men. The prize sailed in their wake, conforming to their movements. All the things had to be done to order and tradition, the masts cock-a-bill as the bodies in their hammocks with the roundshot at their feet were slid overboard to the roll of a drum. Most of the wounded would follow. That seemed to be the fate of life, a scratch and you died, weakness was a trick of the devil, and the ship had still to be run and sailed and the watches to be kept.

During that passage back to England, Fox found himself in a strange mood. During all the years of his service since the beginning of the war in 1793 he had been unable to get back into the swing of Naval life as he had known it before he'd been laid off, as he had then thought for the rest of his life. Were all superior officers nincompoops, quite able to run a ship, to steer her and know if she was clean and smart and if the first lieutenant was up to his job, brave and fearless and devoted to their service, but hopeless when it came to the higher faculties, the strategy and tactics of war, the seizing of the tail of an opportunity to do great things?

Not everyone could be a Drake or a Frobisher or a Blake. The man Fox most often thought about was Sir Clowdisley Shovell. He'd risen from cabin boy to be an admiral, commander of a fleet, victor in sea battles—and to die miserably shipwrecked in his flagship *Association* off the Scillies.

Well, Fox was standing with one foot on the first rung of the ladder. He was a lieutenant. Once he got his step, once he was posted captain, once he obtained his three years' seniority, he, too, would be an admiral. He, too, would fly his flag.

Shovell had died ninety years ago. But Fox was alive, here and now, the blood coursing through his veins—alive, filled with energy and a driving ambition to make his way in the service just so he could grab that much more money for the family. He'd stomach all these titled idiots and submit to their insolences and their scorn; one day he'd fly his own flag, and he'd look up at it and think that it flew there only to bring him in a greater share of prize money for the family.

Despite their reduced manpower and the damage they had sustained they made a good passage and Fox felt that strange lilting jump of the heart when he heard the lookout in the maintop sing out: 'Land ho!'

Soon he could make out the land dead ahead in the afternoon sunlight, the harsh Staddon Heights, and Mount Edgcumbe, and then the roofs of Plymouth rose into view and the Sound and all the busy shipping and they were gliding in under reduced sail. The necessary formalities were quickly gone through and they could pick up their moorings and take that final careful check of the ship that everything had been done that should have been done. Cuthbert Rowlands had trained young Fox hard; he would never shake off the influence that drove him to strive for the utmost perfection and never be content with less.

Duchess was still in commission and, as anyway the hands would never be allowed ashore, some measures were taken to give them a semblance of being in port. The watchbills would have to be filled again. Fox resigned himself to the prospect of fresh raids. Captain Struthers knew by experience that Fox was an exceedingly ruthless and efficient leader of Press Gangs.

The bumboats clustered around *Duchess* and fresh fruit and vegetables were chaffered for through the nettings. No women were allowed aboard, for the ship was still in Commission and as soon as her splinters were sanded down, fresh spars brought aboard, her supplies topped up, she would be off again on her Channel patrol.

Haines came back on board with his prize crew, flushed and with a tendency to crow over his successful navigation of the prize back to port. Fox let him burble away to Beckworth. His own opinion he kept to himself. He knew that Haines would never forget the deadly insult offered him just before they'd boarded *Mortagne*.

The news of the mutiny at the Nore saddened Fox. All shipping was at a standstill in the Thames. The army had been sent in and two regiments manned the shore. Both sides had reached a pitch of bitterness. The government had removed all navigational aids from the river, beacons, buoys, lights and landmarks, so as to prevent the mutineers from sailing out. The men still protested their loyalty to King George, although short-sighted politicians tried to brand the mutineers as Jacobins. Strict watch was kept on the Navy—where next would the infection break out?

As for *Duchess,* her turn would come, for Struthers was not the man to forget what had happened in the estuary of the Laronne. Fox would remember it for the taking of *Mortagne;* Struthers for the abortive mutiny.

Momentarily, Fox expected to see boatloads of red-coated marines put off from shore to board them and take every last man aboard off to gaol to await trial.

In the meantime the men were kept busy. The jury-rigged maintopmast came down and then, as so often infuriatingly happened, the dockyard sent out a foretopmast. Struthers irritatedly told Fox to go ashore and sort out the difficulty.

'I don't care if you take all night!' Struthers raged. 'Don't come back until you have a maintopmast, Mr Fox.'

CHAPTER EIGHT

Fox sat with his feet out-thrust, his back comfortably wedged up against the corner of the settle. He rolled the thick glass of rum between his palms and allowed himself to luxuriate in the sensuous feel and the anticipatory delight. He had chosen to come up here and find a cosy inn out of the hurly-burly of the dock area. Every now and then Fox liked to withdraw into himself, to let the rest of the world go hang, to be just himself, isolated and aloof, and yet still the shrewd observer—he would have gone on with that train of thought to say: the shrewd observer of the world's follies, had he not been too painfully aware of his own follies and inadequacies.

Around him the potroom of the inn closed him in with a mellow comfort; the prints on the walls, the heavy old panelling, the low-beamed roof, the wink and shine of brass and copper ornaments, the sanded floor—all gave him a weird and pseudo-nostalgic impression of what a landsman's life was like. He was realist enough to know that only those with money to jingle in their pockets ever enjoyed the good things of life. There were poor starving wretches outside, mere slips of girls in soiled finery ready to sell themselves, men broken in battle or in the mills, desperate for a crust, young lads seeking to make their way, women growing old and care-worn and past their wits' end to know how to feed their children. But, just for the moment, Fox could pretend they did not exist. Just for this betraying hour of self-indulgence he could sit in his corner with his glass of rum and let the cares of the world flow past without seeking to put his oar in.

The business at the dockyard had gone so disastrously wrong it had given him this heaven-sent opportunity for idleness. Don't come back without the spar, Struthers had said, and the dockyard had thrown up their collective hands in despair and then threatened with Fox's grimmest look, had promised the maintopmast for the morning. How they got the thing Fox didn't care. He'd ship it out to *Duchess* and no doubt rig it himself; that was for the morrow.

A party of young men and women burst in, strangely out of place in the inn. By their clothes, all laces and tucks and bows and skin-tight breeches and satin coats, Fox could see they were well pro-vided with the staff of life—and they intended to disport themselves tonight. They talked with that high nasal glottal affectation that so amused Fox despite his own perfect imitation of it. There was a young man with a leonine head and heavy slumber-ous eyelids the others addressed as 'My Lord', there was a captain of Dragoons in glistening scarlet, there was a young girl in a simple high-waisted white dress, there was an older, darker, more lush woman whose eyes had taken in Fox along with every other man in the room the moment the party had entered. The third man, also a civilian, the others called Sir John, had about him the look of a rake, a professional gambler, a dangerous man. Fox felt the flickering of desire. He did not belong in that company, rakehells coaching down to perdition. He would find his own hell his own way.

But it seemed to be in the nature of these things, as the men began gambling they automatically seized on Fox as, being a naval officer, the only other gentleman in their slumming progress. He felt disinclined to humour them. One of the reasons he had left the dock area was that he had played a few hands with some fellow officers on like errands to his own, and had lost the few guineas in his pocket. He had but one left; and that was to pay for his board and his rum.

He wanted nothing to do with these people. Now they had broken the carefully constructed fabrication of his thoughts the agonised bitterness of what Captain Struthers had told him just before he left the ship overwhelmed him once more.

The situation was simple. Simple and unfair and painful and commonplace.

Because of the successful action and the taking of *Mortagne,* the first lieutenant of *Duchess* was getting his step. As a kind of incidental to the news, Beckworth's father had died, and so now Charles

Beckworth was the Earl of Lymm. He was being posted captain and would, without doubt, immediately obtain a command. That was fine as far as Fox was concerned. He gripped his rum glass more tightly as he thought of how gullible he had been. With Beckworth gone he would be free of the man and at the same time would be the first lieutenant of *Duchess*. Then! One more action like the last— and it would be Captain Fox!

Struthers had told him, with a regret Fox had been in no mood to appreciate, that he was taking a son of his old friend, Admiral Lessingham, as his new first lieutenant. Influence—influence at work again in the Navy had dashed all Fox's hopes. Officers were appointed through influence and not through merit; Fox was a nobody, and nobodies were there to be stepped on by their betters.

'Demme if I don't declare the feller's an outsider,' came the voice of the gallant dragoon captain.

Fox dragged his mind away from thoughts that were blacker than the captain's boots. He had not cared to take his pillaged Spanish sword with him on a mere visit to the dockyard; now he felt thankful he had not. The temptation just to bash this red-coat over the head might have carried him away. He felt a sudden breeze of enjoyment at the thought.

'Look at him,' said the blond-headed Lord. 'Steel buckles to his shoes, and those stockings are never silk, and as for the breeches—' He laughed affectedly. 'They'd suit a coachman and four, I shouldn't wonder.'

This witticism drew answering guffaws from the men and giggles from the women.

Fox kept that withdrawn look on his face. He decided what he would do. He looked up, suddenly, as though coming out of a doze, and put all the force of his dark personality into his words, fashioned around an exact imitation of those noble lords' and ladies' intonations.

'My pardon, gentlemen. I am afraid I did not catch what you had the courtesy to address to me. I have lately come ashore—shipwreck, action, blood, and death—God's death!—and I have been forced to borrow these poor clothes from a dead man and am too fatigued to carry myself to a tailor. Although,' he added this with a dash of spice very enjoyable to him, 'I doubt me there are any tailors worthy of the name outside St James's.'

That had set their sails aback.

The raffish hawk-faced rakehell cocked an eye at the dark-haired woman. She pouted at him, her lips very red.

'A sea battle!' she said, her voice like molasses. 'Please, I pray you, sir, tell us of this action in which I feel sure you were the hero of the hour.'

They weren't hooked yet. Fox had to play them along, tickle them like fat trout, lavishly flatter and act prodigiously; but he took his part with a sudden gaiety that might have betrayed him had his central purpose been less dark and secretive and powerful.

He could string a whole squadron of anecdotes together, could George Abercrombie Fox; the powder monkey of the American Revolutionary War, and the middy of the earlier conflict with France and Spain than this present struggle, the storms at sea, the wild crashings of the broadsides, the blood and maiming, the thrilling headlong dash of the boarding party with, naturally, himself at the head with hundred guinea presentation sword wet with blood.

'Lieutenant George Abercrombie, at your service,' he said, with a smile he knew was so sweet it would have caused the lower deck of *Duchess* to vomit in horrified surprise.

When cards were suggested, and this was the original purpose, Fox was altogether ready to oblige his new acquaintances. He felt a pang of disappointment when *vingt-et-un* was suggested; but he acquiesced cheerfully. He preferred something a little more scientific; but this would serve his purpose as well.

As a stranger to them he was allowed the first deal and, being Fox, he saw to it that when shuffling he put the cards into a convenient sequence. He blind cut, and then dealt. It could hardly be called winning, that first hand; Fox knew where the cards were that fell on the table and he knew that he would take into his grasp the golden guineas lavished upon the bets.

The women took part as well, and this might once have surprised him; but women had changed much since the war. They were more independent, more mannish in some ways, the difficulties and shortages making them make do and mend—in his sailor's phrase—so that they shed much of the older image of womenkind as being soft and pliant and helpless. But in other ways they were more feminine than ever. Fox caught himself as the women threw off their cloaks. Their sheer muslin gowns were as near transparent as might be; distinctly he could see the dark circles of the aureoles and the sheen of pink of the nipples as their breasts thrust against the thin material. This evening might be warmer than he had expected.

He played carefully. He did not let himself win too much too often; and he made great play when he lost, in his affected voice complaining how bad a player he was. Still, his deft manipulation of the cards, learned through many hours solitary practice, enabled him to dictate the way of the game. He was cheating them. He revelled in it. Where he had played absolutely fairly with his brother officers, he would cheat as much as he dared with these sprigs of the nobility. Anyway, those officers sent on dockyard duty were men like himself, the drudges of superiors too high and mighty ever to descend to the hard practicalities of naval routine.

He well knew the risks he was running. But the game demanded little skill; simply bare-faced nerve. With a run of good hands in his favour he found himself twenty guineas the richer in as many minutes of play.

To a man like Fox scrupulous honesty was demanded and given in any dealings with his equals and those set beneath him in the hierarchy of the Navy. To those in authority over him he would give loyalty and scrupulous honesty when it came to naval matters; but to dandies like this, landsmen whose contempt of him still showed like thorns dragged across his flesh, scions of the aristocracy for whom he had only contempt, he would give all the wiles of his cunning nature. He would cheat them; yes; and be damned to them.

Let them think about how they took their money; the sweatshops, the mills, the rolling acres with their tumble-down insanitary cottages, the poor men's endless work and suffering, the consumptive children, the ground-down women. He had no compunction in redistributing a little wealth, had George Abercrombie Fox; and if he burned for it in the hereafter that was a small price to pay for what good he could do here and now on this earth.

'Demme! The cards ain't runnin' my way tonight!'

The lion-headed man, Lord Coylton, threw down his knave and ten which skidded across Fox's just-turned-up five, three, four, two and seven. The dark-haired woman, Clara, murmured a sympathy the malicious look in her eyes belied. Fox raked in Coylton's guineas; on twenty he'd bet heavily. Captain Flaxton grunted and crossed one immaculately-breeched leg over the other. Fox winced; that fine-drawn stitching would surely start and split from knee to buttock. Lady Frances, the slender girl whose face held no indication whatsoever to her character, asked Paul Linton, the rakehell with the devil's face, if he would be so kind as to order up more port.

'The evenin's beginnin' to wear on me, God's tooth,' she said, yawning.

Linton took that as an open invitation. Fox had summed up the party. The captain had been added as a last minute invitation and had no part in the later doings planned for the coaching trip. Linton and Lady Frances clearly had an understanding. Fox had no wish to pry into the secrets behind this meeting, this drinking and gambling in a low Plymouth inn. If their families frowned on the match, illicit love-making would go on. As for Clara and Lord Coylton, Fox had been getting ideas there.

Presently, when on the table before him a heap of gold proclaimed fifty juicy guineas that were his for the taking, the gambling broke up. What was fifty guineas to these people? A nothing, a bagatelle, not enough to keep one of the women in gloves. But to Fox it was half the sum he hoped he might receive for boarding *Mortagne,* for risking his life and limb, for taking risks such as these popinjays read of in their 'Morning Post' with such delicious shudders, quite unable to imagine the reality.

He made polite goodnights, smiling, speaking with that high affected intonation, wishing them a good night's sleep, hiding his smiles as he felt the weight of the gold in his pockets. The landlord of the inn heaved a sigh of relief and began to bustle the maid about to clear away the glasses and the pots, to collect up the cards, to sweep the floor.

On an impulse Fox took out a guinea and gave it to the girl. She looked up at him beneath her mob cap, her smudgy face frightened, her snub nose wet.

'I ain't a bad girl, sir, beggin' your pardon—'

Fox felt the thrill of anger and agony shoot through him. 'Of course you're not,' he said, roughly. 'I never thought it. Can't I say I think you—'

He knew it was excessive; but she was a fellow creature.

She took the guinea, still looking at him fearfully. He turned away, too case-hardened to be hurt; but feeling all the misery and squalor of small people's lives enmeshing him.

It would be strange to sleep in a bed. It would be strange to sleep in a bed that did not heave and surge and wallow. He stripped off his breeches and stockings that had given such amusement to the noble lord, hung his coat on the stand, ruffled out his sleeves, and, with the fifty guineas in his purse snugged to his waist, turned in. He had not come prepared for cardplaying. His full sleeves had been empty; the little pistol he habitually carried still with his duffle aboard *Duchess*. He had not noticed its lack tonight, although normally he felt as naked without that little gun as without his folded kerchief.

He blew out the candle, not bothering with the snuffer and lay back. A stealthy scratching sounded at his door. He sat up. Tomorrow night he would be back aboard the ship; this one night ashore was precious; now, perhaps, came the item missing from the inventory.

He opened the door to admit Clara, wrapped in a peignoir, who padded on naked feet into the room and immediately climbed into the bed. She had not said a word.

Fox was aroused, there was no doubt about that. This Clara was a full-bodied, dark and luscious woman. Her red lips curved with a wanton smile of invitation and he knew now he had not misread her signals during cards.

'And milord Coylton?' he said, the irony kept hidden below the surface, like the deadly body of a shark when only its dorsal fins shows.

'The fool dropped dead asleep on me, God's blood, the minute we were abed.' She lifted the covers invitingly. 'Do you get in, George, and warm me, for it's hot I am and hotter I'd be—'

She snuggled back as Fox cocked a leg and slid into the bed. She removed her peignoir herself, tossed it carelessly on to the floor. Fox, determined not to miss anything, laboriously struck flint and steel, relit the candle. Clara's dark hair lay on the pillow like a flood of ebony, a wave in the midnight sea. He put out a hand and touched her. Her body was feverishly hot. She pulled the nightgown away from her throat and now he could see those full breasts whose outlines he had devoured beneath the transparent modish dress.

She laughed, a deep gurgle in her throat.

She lifted her white arms for him.

Something stuck then, for George Abercrombie Fox. This woman took what she wanted from life. The noble lord had fallen asleep on her, stupified with the brandy he'd drunk. Her womanly body had been aroused in anticipation and now here she was, ready to take from Fox. For he saw that clearly enough. He might take her; but in reality it was she who would be taking from him.

Anything they wanted, they took, these upper-crusty superiors of his. Well, this one wouldn't take his manhood. She smiled more widely, and now her hands dropped down and stroked his chest through the opened neck of his shirt. Her hands trickled over his body like spiders, the scent of her hair like musk filled his nostrils. Despite himself he took her breasts and cupped them, fondling, squeezing—he pulled back.

'George? What's the matter?'

'No,' he said. He spoke hoarsely. He had to force the words out. A sailor man took a woman when he could, where he could, how he could. But for a sailorman like Fox this woman was sundered from him not so much by class, or money, or position; but by the animosity he bore all her breed. What if she knew he was a mere penniless second lieutenant, without birth or breeding, a product of the London slums, a marshboy, without prospects in the Navy —without even a paltry sword of honour patronisingly bestowed by a grateful and mercenary Patriotic Fund?

The conceit made him chuckle. He could do without this white flesh.

He got out of bed, pulled her out by the arm, slapped her on the rump.

'Go back to Coylton,' he said. Her bewilderment and then her anger could do nothing to move him. He felt a sudden pity for her. 'Clara—Clara—you are a woman any man would give riches to possess—'

She stared at him, her breasts heaving in the opened nightdress, her colour flaming, her dark hair swirling about her shoulders.

'You devil!' The candle flame caught in her eyes so that they flared scarlet at him. 'D'you call yourself a man? What are you, like them all in the Navy? I know your kind—'

He would not hear any more. He opened the door, brusquely, moving with a jerkiness that worried him. Already he knew his left eye was closing up on him; wide open it yet revealed little of the room, of the woman, to him.

'Good night, Clara,' he said.

She flung herself past him. Her bare feet hit the wooden floor softly, like fresh meat on a slab, quite unlike the horny patter of seamen called on deck. He chuckled at the thought. He closed the door softly. At that, she had had a nice shape. He'd remember that.

Stupid bitch. A lady of the land, thought she could buy and sell him as she might some poor deluded peasant on her broad acres . . . His thoughts were muzzy. He slept.

He turned out late deliberately the following morning and then felt annoyance at his lift of relief when the servant girl told him the milords and ladies had left. He looked at the girl, Sue, with her smudgy face and gawky mob cap and sagging breasts in the sloppy bodice. She'd called herself a good girl, not a bad girl. God help us, thought George Abercrombie Fox, there were few enough of those left in these roaring days of war.

He took himself off to the dockyard after a shave and breakfast and found the maintopmast still not available.

He roared around the dock offices kicking up blazes until he secured a promise that the mast would be ready late that evening. He breathed deeply. Corruption and graft had still not been eliminated from the Navy's shore facilities; no doubt one day it would be entirely eradicated. Come the day, prayed Fox.

There had been cases of captains supposed to equip their ships with eighteen-pounders thankfully taking nine-pounders just so they could get to sea. Fox was a firm believer in big long range guns. He deplored the Navy's attitude to sights, although well aware of the futility of using them with the guns currently available. He had a soft spot for big carronades, the invention from Carron, in Scotland, that could mount a large calibre gun on a sliding carriage instead of a trucked one; but carronades because of their necessarily light construction were of short range. What Fox wanted was an accurate long twenty-four-pounder. With that and a gun's crew he had drilled and trained up himself, he could feel confident. He sometimes thought he might go for a thirty-two-pounder if he could ensure a really rapid rate of fire. As it was, he must plod along with the Navy and sail in yard arm to yard arm and blast away like two pugilists toeing the line.

He bought himself a bite to eat at three o'clock

—Navy habits died hard. A plate of beef, some bread and cheese, two tankards of local ale. He felt better after that.

He patted his waistline. He had nothing to fear there if he ate Navy rations; ashore in five or ten years he'd be as fat and bloated as a cartoon figure from one of this Thomas Rowlandson's savage caricatures of life.

He saw a number of parties of seamen, headed by tough-faced lieutenants, all well-armed with cudgels and bludgeons, moving about and guessed the press was out again in force. Looking out over the water of the Hamoaze he could see two seventy-fours readying for sea, a three decker heading their line, and a couple of frigates besides *Duchess. Thunderer* was gone—he remembered his brush with that ninny Lieutenant Cathcart, and *Tremendous* still had the garlands, suspended now from her three masts which had all been keeled in. The fuss of shore boats about her and the other ships amused Fox. Here he was, an officer, free to walk about in his uniform, shabby though it was, whilst those men he commanded in action were forcibly penned up aboard their ships and firmly refused all opportunities of going ashore. Mind you, if a seaman ran it was one way of making sure he got his pay. He risked a thousand lashes, too, into the bargain.

Towards evening he discovered, on returning to the dockyard, that the maintopmast was still not ready. There had been a tremendous log jam. He cursed. Struthers would begin to wonder what had happened to his second lieutenant. Despite Struthers' orders—given, he had to admit, in the heat of the moment—he felt it prudent to go aboard *Duchess* and report. Struthers would explode in bad temper and put all the blame personally on Fox; but that was a normal hazard of the service.

He felt like a long long drink of rum. No British sailor could be trusted with alcohol in normal circumstances; Fox, as an officer, quite clearly could. That was one of the differences between officers and lower deck men. He rolled into an inn, snuffing the mingled scents of sawdust and rum and horses and rum and human sweat and rum, and espying a group of shabbily-dressed naval officers joined them with his glass and idly talked away a couple of hours. Struthers like himself could wait.

Like himself they were about dockyard business although one, a long lean saturnine individual, a lieutenant with more years behind him than ahead, was astonishingly, all things considered, on half pay and awaiting a ship. They talked about the usual details of the service, of the successes in single ship actions to which everyone's eyes turned, they talked about women and, of little interest to Fox, of horses, of the scandals at court hinted at in broadsheets and pamphlets, of the ruinous taxes the landlubbers bemoaned. A full roistering life went on ashore, a life strange to Fox like life on the West Coast of Africa, both foreign to him yet a part of his own life.

The rum was beginning to get to him now, he was thinking of Clara, the fullness of her, the scent of her hair, the feel of her. What kind of a fool had he been? Didn't he need a woman? The officers were talking about the recent great battle off Cape St Vincent—not a single one of them had so much as mentioned the Nore mutiny, here, ashore in a waterfront inn—one of the lieutenants having served aboard *Excellent.* He was explaining, as though no one had ever heard the story before, of how Commodore Nelson following *Excellent* in *Captain* when Collingwood stood off in chase, had used the Spanish *San Nicholas* to board the Spanish first rate, *San Josef.*

' "Nelson's Patent Boarding Bridge" they're calling it now,' the *Excellent's* lieutenant said, with a hiccough.

'So,' said Fox, downing his rum and swinging for the door, all the remembered thunder of the broadsides in his ears, 'So I've heard.' He reeled where he stood. He needed a woman.

The lieutenant lifted an eyebrow. 'Do I take it, sir, that you also had the honour to serve in the general action?'

'Honour?' said Fox, making a valiant attempt to remain upright, the taproom whirling about him. 'Honour? My seamen are due £4 5s. 0d, prize money for the battle. That's the kind of honour I understand.'

As though negotiating the starboard companionway in a gale of wind, Fox staggered towards the door, luffed up hard, let fly his sheets and fell out into the yard where the darkness dropped about him. He relieved himself up against a wall and the action reminded him of why he had left the cosy taproom. He stared about owlishly. It was dark, infernally dark, and that thrice-confounded maintopmast ought to be ready now. He blundered off down an alley where the wind racketted past him. He didn't hear a thing until a foot slithered at his back. He half-turned and saw the upraised arm and the cudgel and then he awoke in the gutter, his head pealing like a chime of bells, his body shivering with the cold.

He was dressed in just his shirt. A wet-stickiness at the back and side of his head felt like tacky blood. Everything was gone—shoes, uniform, hat, money—everything.

He groaned and tried to stand up. Footpads had done this to him, desperate men, criminals, men who had taken his money. He remembered vaguely, with a twinge, how he had gained that purse of gold; he had stolen it, really, and now it had been stolen from him. The poetic justice of the thing did not appeal to George Abercrombie Fox—not one little bit, it didn't.

He stood up and heaved a bit, the sickness would wear off along with the drunkenness; but his head was going to ache for a long time yet.

The inn must be back there. If those sailor comrades of his were still there . . . Sailor comrades they would prove to be, right enough; they would look after him, even the *Excellent*'s lieutenant, who had regarded him with great disfavour. He moved along the alley, blundering, and the alley was filled with shapes in rushing motion. A man seized him by the arm, swung him around. Another man grunted and his whiskers scraped Fox's cheek as he shouted back over his shoulder.

'Here's one, sir. Belay there, you lubber! You're acomin' along o' us!'

Fox knew. He straightened up with great dignity.

'Belay that, you blagskite! I'm a King's Officer!'

The man's laugh sounded full and hearty. 'A King's Horficer, is it! Then you'll welcome a nice sail! Come hup, my beauty!'

The Press Gang clustered about Fox now. A midshipman crisped an order, the whole mass was in motion again. Fox was forced to run with them.

'I'm a King's Officer!' he yelled again. He struggled. 'You benighted fools! Avast, curse you! I'll have every man of you triced up and flogged, you o—' And he went into a lurid string of seaman's oaths well known and frequently used on the lower deck. All his marshboy and powder monkey invective poured out.

'This 'un's a catch, sir!' shouted the man gripping his bicep in a grip like a carpenter's vice. 'A prime seaman or I'm a lobster!'

'You'll have a redder back than a lobster, you lubber, if you don't let me go!'

A lieutenant turned, all cocked hat and impatient profile. He snapped a savage order.

'Keep that man quiet, bo's'n!'

'Aye, aye, sir.'

Fox yelled and tried to run and for the second time that night the sky fell in on him and blackness took him for its own.

123

CHAPTER NINE

His Britannic Majesty's ship *Tiger* was a ninety-eight gun three-decker, with thirty-two-pounders on the lower gun deck, twenty-four-pounders on the second gun-deck and twelve-pounders above that. She had sixty-eight-pound smashers on her forecastle, and she was the bustling home of a thousand men. In the admiral's cabin aft his high and mightiness Vice-Admiral Sir Blundesely Creighton, K.C.B. could survey with a just pride the flagship and the three seventy-fours that formed the rest of his squadron. In the captain's cabin Captain Sir John Pulteney R.N. was concerned to make his ship the most efficient and pleasant flagship the admiral had ever sailed in, and he made it very clear to his first lieutenant, and the rest of his officers, that he intended they should do everything in their power to maintain that high resolve. In their turn the officers bore down on the warrant officers, who chased the petty officers, who flicked around at the seamen, who, passing on the kicks, saw to it that the landsmen and boys knew who really manned the ship, by God!

One thousand men in a floating wooden home a hundred and eighty feet long on the longest deck, and fifty feet wide, posed problems of man management. Eight hundred and fifty was the proper complement; but the Press Gangs had been out, and there were extra marines aboard, for the gallant Sir Blundesely Creighton had schemes to hatch which needed men. Following the squadron of ships of the line sailed a motley collection of frigates, sloops, brigs and cutters.

A thousand men—and one of those men was George Abercrombie Fox.

His first words on regaining consciousness had been: *'Not again!'*

His head hurt. The repeated blows he had been struck still echoed in his head with the beat of his blood. He felt dizzy. He remembered little of the processes whereby he found himself regulated as a landsman aboard *Tiger*. When he had proved himself he might be re-rated a seaman; but speed had the squadron in its grip, everyone infected by the passion of the admiral to set sail.

The days passed for Fox in an unpleasant daze. A daze of days. He did what he was told and retained enough of his expertise to avoid most of the tortures suffered by the inexperienced caught up by the press. As the orders 'All hands ahoy!' and 'All hands holystone decks!' and the infuriating call of the boatswain's pipes, on this large ship reinforced by calls twittering from boatswain's mates in every

126

corner of the ship, sounded, he could usually summon up interest enough to do some artful dodging and escape most of the holystoning. One of the petty officers thought it particularly fine to yell at the top of his lungs the old rousting out call in full: 'Out or down, there; out or down, there! Rouse out! Rouse out! Rouse out! Lash and carry, lash and carry, show a leg or else a purser's stocking. Rouse and shine, rouse and shine! *Lash up and stow!* It's tomorrow morning and the sun's scorching your bloody eyes out!' He sometimes varied the last perjorative; but the sense remained the same.

Half-asleep in the cold of the dawnlight the men would scramble out, coughing and hacking, their eyes, runny and inflamed, looking for the quickest exits onto the deck and to avoid the rattans and the starters. They'd carry their hammocks up (Fox rolled his with its regulation seven lashings with a remembered pang) and stow them in the hammocks nettings lining the rails. Pumps would be rigged and the holystoning of the decks could begin. Breakfast, a long way off still, would follow the cleaning of weapons. The first lieutenant was a tartar. The petty officers used their starters freely. Fox endured. Each time he tried to explain he was an officer too, he would be thumped back. Approaching an officer he knew would be difficult; there was all the difference between a frigate and a three decker. The officers remained remote to a landsman who was chased by the able seamen.

As the boatswain's mate who had been among

the press gang told him, with a wide mocking smile: 'You—a ship's horficer! An' I brung you aboard in your shirt, roaring drunk, dragged from the gutter! A likely story, my lad, a likely story!' The petty officer chuckled and flicked his starter around Fox's rump. 'A single look at you, you lubber, 'd tell anyone you's no gennelman, no, nor a horficer either!'

'But,' protested Fox, 'I know about ships—I can tell you your duties word for word—'

The boatswain's mate puffed up at that. Fox realised he had tried the wrong tack; but it was too late now.

'That's enuff o' that, you blagskite! You been to sea afore, I c'n tell that! Indiaman, most likely—or mebbe you've served King George before and ran —eh, how's that for size?' And the starter flicked again.

The most important bell of the day came at twelve-thirty—one bell. That was when grog was piped. Fox despised himself for falling into the men's habits of living from grog to grog. He tended to think of this period in his life in terms of 'affairs'. He was a prisoner. He was as much a prisoner as though he had been captured by the French or the Spanish and was mewed up in some stone cell with iron bars. He was mewed up in a wooden prison, with iron guns and iron officers and iron discipline.

There was the affair of the cat.

The complete skeleton of a cat was discovered when a barrel of salt beef was opened, the meat in its grisly toughness and unrecognisability lifted straight from the brine and there was the cat's skeleton. The meat was a good twenty years old, it could have been loaded and unloaded from ship after ship and have sailed five times around the world for all the purser knew—or cared. The men divided into two camps; those who declared the cat to have got into the salt beef in the normal course of its processing and the other faction who said it was self-evident the cat had got into the barrel alive and been battened down.

Much acrimony flourished; the skeleton was in perfect shape, so how could it have been processed? demanded the second school—and—show us the mouse skeleton and we'll believe you, cried the first.

However the cat had got into the barrel, the beef was still piled into the caldrons and cooked for hours on end to junk. The biscuits issued were maggotty, which was a relief, the hard and brittle insects into which the maggots would turn being bitter to the taste. The cheeses could have been used, almost, as trucks for the masts, as was the custom in the old navy, and only the pea soup gave little cause for complaint.

There was the affair of the hanging man. Fox helped to cut him down and looked with a feeling he supposed must be pity on the twisted features, the distended eyes and bitten tongue. But the man had been a weakling. Blockade duty must end, one day, when the war was over, even if that day might lie decades in the future.

There was the affair of the captain's goat; but Fox had the sense to steer clear of that one. The culprits were never found and Fox, had he been given a choice, would have plumped for the young gentlemen of the gunroom, although some of the afterguard wore the sleek look of goat-milk fed enthusiasts.

There was the affair of *Tapperton*, a smart thirty-two gun frigate which almost fell on board of *Tiger* and was fended off with a smashed bowsprit and dangling jibs and whose fancy figurehead was so rapidly pillaged by the watch on deck only a drab wooden stump could ever be found to be returned to an infuriated frigate captain.

The small craft which had sailed out with the squadron had now dispersed to independent cruises, pursued by the jealous invective of those unfortunates condemned to blackade duty, and what with gales and beating up and beating down, Fox grew wearied with time and labour. His lassitude of spirit came from a deep understanding of his character that this was really where he belonged. He was reaping his just reward. How dare he aspire to being an officer? Him—a piece of floating scum? This was his milieu, a lower deck hand aspiring to become an able seaman, to avoid a flogging, to get what grog he could of anyone foolish enough to part with it. He couldn't even laugh in the presence of an officer; that was punishable by the lash. A captain could in theory only order up to twelve strokes; in practice he gave what he thought the miscreant deserved.

Yes, George Abercrombie Fox had sunk to his rightful place.

But he did take note of *Tiger*'s points of sailing, and found her to be less stumpy and unweatherly than most of this breed of three-deckers. Oh, she was no *Victory* with her superb sailing qualities; but she was quicker through the water with the wind on her quarter than any of the seventy-fours in the squadron with her.

Fox felt particularly cut off from news from wider horizons. Whatever had been the admiral's original haste, that had passed without anything to show for it. The days wore on. This was the great year of mutinies; it was also the great year of prisons, as far as Fox was concerned.

When at last the monotony was broken Fox had to make a conscious effort to rouse himself from the mental lethargy that had enveloped him. His body had been extraordinarily active, but his mind had slumbered, stupified. If *Duchess* was to sail up over the horizon and Captain Struthers was to come aboard to the twitter of pipes Fox couldn't really see what he could do. He was that far gone in apathy. A real officer, a real gentleman, would have found a way to have proclaimed his identity. Fox felt himself suspended in that hateful limbo between his origins and his aspirations.

During this whole period his eye had not troubled him.

The break came with the shrill of pipes and the flicking of rope's ends and the measured tramp of booted feet as the marines paraded. As a man who could pull an oar, Fox would be going in the cutter commanded by Lieutenant Gloag, an ill-tempered Scotsman with a jaundiced face and a tongue like a ripsaw. As an oarsman, Fox would be told what to do, issued with a cutlass and a pistol, and then expected not to think but to fight and kill and obey—always to obey instantly and without the fatal hesitation produced by thought processes.

'It's *Narcissus,*' the cutter's coxswain told them as he inspected their pistols and cutlasses, with an eye to cleanliness, the state of the flints, the sharpness of the cutlass blades. 'A thirty-six gun frigate. I ain't never heard on her—any o' you scally wags?'

The boat's crew had not. All that was known was that a British frigate, *Narcissus,* was lying in Ancre roadstead beneath the frowning guns of the fort, flying French colours over British. That was an intolerable state of affairs and must be remedied instantly. A cutting-out expedition would teach the Frogs to capture British ships.

Fox found himself fuming and fretting over his own ignorance. As an officer he would have been party to the discussions, the planning of details, the organisation. He would have been commanding this boat, instead of sitting on a thwart and hauling an oar.

A miraculous change came over *Tiger.* All the sullen looks vanished. The spirit-breaking monotony of blockade was in its turn to be broken; the prospect of action gave everyone a tremendous lift of spirits. As a three-decker *Tiger* could not approach too close and the boats would be towed in by the *Poppy,* brig, and the *Rosinante,* cutter. The boom would be taken care of by the launch, the cutters would push through and the gigs would see to the cables. Everyone could guess the general outlines of the plan. But the seamen were entrusted with their own individual tasks, and no more. This was planned in the conventional cutting-out expedition way. Fox found, suddenly, that he could breathe again, as though something had been lifted from his spirit that freed his mind.

He breathed in and swelled out his massive chest and for the first time he filled the clothes issued from the slop chest. He fingered the cutlass and pistol. This, by Old Harry, was it!

Because of this desire to get to grips with the enemy, which he could recognise as his desire to have the opportunity to strike out at anyone to release the tensions tying him up, he was not too critical of the preparations. His alert mind had slumbered too long on the lower deck. *Narcissus,* of which he had never heard, was just a thirty-six gun frigate to be cut out. That probably meant, in the way of naval gunnery nomenclature, that she carried more than forty guns, perhaps as many as forty-four; *Duchess* being called a thirty-two and being armed with exactly thirty-two broadside guns had been the exception rather than the rule. Fox just fingered his cutlass and pistol and hungered for the moment when his feet hit the deck and he could go into action and release the anger stifling him.

The Navy was in some respects like one huge

family. It was strange that the seamen had among them no-one who knew *Narcissus*. They'd know up on the quarterdeck all the particulars of the ship; those details would find their way down to the lower deck in time; they weren't really necessary for men whose duty was to obey in their killing.

The night chosen for the attack that was to cutout *Narcissus* was black, without a moon and with a mantle of cloud covering the stars. Fox thought of the lieutenant whose task it would be to navigate them into the frigate lying in the Ancre roadstead. As a piece of seamanship it would be interesting, considered Fox, something he would have joyed in doing well. *Poppy* and *Rosinante* collected their brood of boats, amid much muttered cursing everything was sorted out; as the sails filled with the wind, light southerly and just right for the work in hand, the whole flotilla moved towards the land leaving *Tiger* to brace up her yards and under topsails and jib go lolloping away into the offing.

The brig and the big cutter—the single-masted cutter possessed ten six-pounders and a crew of sixty—would release the boats just before the boom and would then lie off ready to bear a hand. Fox did, for a fleeting moment, wonder if it might not have been easier for the boats to have gone in under their own canvas; but he dismissed the thought. Thinking was almost painful to him again, after all these years.

The darkness breathed over the water with a profound effect of breathlessness. At each little noise, from the muffled oars in the rowlocks, from a splash as a wave caught an oarblade, from a pistol or a cutlass chinking, the surrounding silence grew more silent. The water was almost at flood and bore the boats swiftly on with only steady pulling needed to keep them on course, each following the carefully shaded darklantern held over the transom of the boat ahead.

The launch was carrying forty men to tackle the boom.

The cutter commanded by Lieutenant Gloag in which Fox rowed with the steady rhythm essential and habitual under these conditions, contained twenty seamen and ten marines and their duty was to board over the starboard bow. The other cutter was to take the starboard quarter. The gigs, when they had cut the cables, would then join in the attack. The launch, having cleared the boom away, would then come on.

Pulling his oar Fox kept his mind on the business in hand and his eyes inboard. A seaman catching a crab now would be triced up with the leather band around his kidneys and flogged silly at the gratings tomorrow—provided he wasn't killed first over the alarm the crab catching would cause.

They would be forty-two-pounders in the fort. He was reminded of the forty-two-pounders in *Fort du Peuple* when he'd fought *Mortagne* in the estuary of the Laronne. They'd been lucky to have put that fire out so quickly; once fire got even the slimmest of holds aboard a wooden ship with its tarred lines and canvas and its dry-painted wood there was no stopping it. Any minute now the

135

launch would be up to the boom—the officer there would have to be quick and sure, for the French were sure to have a guard boat rowing. Without at first his being aware of it Fox's mind was beginning to stir into motion, like the wheels of a windmill after a prolonged calm.

'Easy.' Gloag's voice reached them in a whisper. The oars barely stirred and the cutter slowed and drifted with the last of the flood. Fox desperately wanted to turn around and look ahead to see what was happening; but he knew the treatment he'd receive if he did that now.

He heard what sounded like the old oaken door of a plague church creaking open on rusted hinges to let out all the ghosts of yesteryear.

He had time to realise it was the sound of the boom being moved when a shout lifted, high and shrill—'*Qui va la?*'

A pistol shot answered.

Abruptly the night was shattered by a musketry volley. Men's voices rose, shouting and bellowing, mingled with a shrill scream of pain.

So much for stealthy surprise!

'Give way!' shouted Gloag. He bent forward with his lemon-coloured face eerily illuminated by the reflected glow of fires and lanterns ahead, beyond Fox's back. 'We're spotted! It's all or nothing now! *Pull like the devil!*'

CHAPTER TEN

The night split apart like a lazarette exploding.

Fox bent double and thrust his oar blade deep, pulled back with all the terrible power of his back muscles and thigh muscles channelled into dragging the oar through the water. The boat's crew responded to the urgent shouts of Mr Gloag; they pulled like very devils.

The boat hit some underwater obstruction, leaped, shivered, then fell back into the water heavily and surged on, the white wash creaming aft all lurid and orange in the flames. The Fort was firing, *Narcissus* was firing, the roadstead lit up like a fireworks display.

Now they were surging past the ruin of the boom. Some projecting underwater spar must have given them that lurch—then Fox saw the remains of the launch, gunwale under, with oarsmen clinging on, their white faces staring up, their mouths black ohs as they shouted unheard in the din of cannon fire.

The cutter's oars rose and fell in a series of neat straight-lined circles of water, stamping past the launch. Fox saw his blade catch some poor devil across the head and fling him back and all Fox could do, bending and pulling, bending and pulling, was pray silently that the man hadn't been killed, would survive.

A gout of white water reared a dozen yards off the weather beam and the southerly wind blew the spray across the cutter. The boat surged on. The middy in the bows was yelling, high-pitched, and Gloag was peering ahead, giving tentative pushes and pulls to the tiller. The marines sat stolidly in the centre, their muskets upright between their knees, a solid block of red in the light and black in the shadows.

The cutter leaped ahead. Shot fell into the sea all about them. Spouts rose like phantoms on either hand, like ghosts swaying above them; and still they rowed with a mechanical frenzy, in, out, in, out, stamping their way across Ancre roadstead to the frigate that was their target.

They passed the other cutter, awash, her crew clinging on and yelling, waving their arms. They could not stop. Gloag roared them on. It was like some eerie regatta in hell, racing men's lives against death that rained down on them in fire and smoke and iron.

Fox daren't look over his shoulder. This whole affair was a botch. Now they passed a gig locked to a big French ten-oared boat. As the two boats swayed together cutlasses clanked and pistols exploded; the middy in command of the gig had gone for the guardboat and Fox could see that dereliction of orders as giving them in the cutter a chance to slip through. Whoever had planned this cutting-out expedition had blundered.

The second gig was going for the anchor cable. Fox could just glimpse her as Gloag swung the tiller over. He, at least, had the sense to disregard his orders and go for the quarterdeck. *Narcissus* was moored head and stern, her larboard facing the shore and her starboard facing out to sea; and from that starboard eighteen-pounders were banging away. A shot ploughed into the sea alongside the cutter and Fox felt as though some gigantic force had smashed upwards through his hands and arms and jolted his head off.

He saw the splintered end of his oar loom white and jagged in the flame-filled darkness. Another eighteen-pounder went off but the flame and shot passed over his head. They were beneath the deepest angle of fire of the guns. Now the Fort had ceased fire; they probably could not see the boats from their eminence and could not fire on them for fear of hitting the frigate. Fox felt a sudden great lift of his spirits.

And then a last shot slapped into the sea close by the bows and toppled the cutter clean over in the water.

Fox was in the sea, swimming instinctively, splashing his way towards the frigate's stern.

He took a mouthful of water, surfaced, spat, shook his head. He grabbed on to the mooring

139

cable and hauled himself up a couple of feet. Gloag was gripping the cable below him and gasping.

'Come hup!' said Fox and reached down and hauled the lieutenant clear of the water.

He crabbed up the cable and put a hand to the frigate's rail. A mess of netting hung down, suspended from the cross jack yard and gaff. Fox drew his cutlass and slashed at it; but the tarred cords merely sagged away. He cursed and hacked again. He heard muskets banging and felt a ball pass his shoulder. He hacked with all the frenzied savagery of a primordial man tearing at a sabre-tooth tiger. He made the beginnings of a hole, enlarged it, thrust his head through and, more by instinct than any reasoning powers, flung himself bodily sideways so that the half-pike buried its point in the oaken timbers beside him. He was snared up like a fly in a spider's web; but another furious assault broke the hole wider and he was able to tumble through.

The pike-wielder had just dragged his weapon free when Fox cut him down. He jumped for the deck where a mass of men awaited him. He drew his pistol, wet it was only an encumbrance, flung it into the midst of them.

He was shouting. He hadn't realised that. His bestial shouts of animal fear and rage were caught up and echoed as Gloag and the men from the overturned cutter followed him through the boarding nettings. He waved the cutlass and it seemed as though a magic wand swept away the clustered men by the taffrail.

Men were at his shoulder now, fighting with him, pressing the French forward towards the wheel. Here a knot of men clumped, muskets flashed, the man beside Fox yelped in a quiet, surprised kind of way, and slid to the deck. Fox jumped forward, caught a French officer by the collar and ran his cutlass through his body. He jerked it free and slashed immediately at a lieutenant who tried to stick him with an elegant little small-sword. Him, Fox hacked down, stepped over the body, slashed into the next group. He was past the wheel now. A fresh series of shouts and cries echoed from forward. The gig's crew must be climbing aboard via the fore chains. Just how many men there were aboard he didn't know; probably a hundred and fifty to two hundred Frenchmen ranged against the less than forty English who had scrambled aboard.

But surprise, heading action, vicious courage, these things were what counted. The French were demoralised; how could the English have survived the cannonade and how could they have possibly cut their way through the nettings?

Fox grabbed a seaman by the shoulder, recognised him as Affleck, stroke oar.

'Get aft and cut the cable, Affleck! There's an axe in a becket there! Lively, now!'

'Aye, aye, sir,' answered Affleck with that automatic response to commands given with that sure touch of authority to which he had been disciplined. He scarcely looked at Fox; he might even have thought it was Gloag giving him the order, or another British officer aboard; whatever he thought he did not hesitate in running back aft to obey the order.

All along the maindeck of the frigate French were still standing to their guns. They had just ceased firing the starboard battery and their ears still rang with the broadsides. Now they waited, stupidly, for orders. They wouldn't get the orders they expected from the quarterdeck; all the French had been cleared from there.

Now was the moment to make a mistake; to hesitate between a headlong charge along the gangways to join up with the English battling on the forecastle, to try to swing a thirty-two pounder carronade around from the quarterdeck to rake the maindeck, or to send men aloft to set sail.

Fox didn't hesitate.

Even as he yelled he saw Lieutenant Gloag limping up to the quarterdeck rail, holding his leg on which a big damp patch shone wetly. The darkness was much lighter now; the clouds were shredding and dissipating and the wind was shifting; if they delayed too long they'd have trouble getting her out of the roadstead.

'Adams, Curtis, you—Stinky—get aloft and set the maintops'l! I'll deal with the Froggies here. Step lively!' He bustled half a dozen men up the ratlines. He couldn't go himself; his job was to make sure the cables were cut, there was a man at the wheel, and see the sheets were hauled home

142

and there were men at the braces to haul the yards around. But first, as soon as the maintopsail dropped free he must get some men on the halliards. At that moment seven marines with their sergeant trotted up. Fox yelled.

'Sergeant—cover those French on the maindeck!' He didn't dare order them to tail on to the halliards; their disciplined fire would be invaluable in covering the main deck. Now Gloag was saying something to him, impatiently, almost querulously.

'Get to the halliards!' Fox shouted. 'Here comes the maintop's'l!'

'I'm in command here, my man!' Gloag was yelling, his lugubrious face savage. 'Get out of my way —I'll have you flogged—'

'Shut up!' screamed Fox. 'I'll trouble you to obey my orders, Mr Gloag, without question! Get aft at once and make sure the cable's cut—she's moving!'

The head of *Narcissus* began to swing. Someone on the forecastle had done a good job. Before Gloag could move the stern moved, and Fox knew she was free.

The marines were firing now; and bodies were tumbling to the maindeck. A musket flashed from down there and a marine staggered back, drunkenly, dropping his musket, his face smashed.

'Belay that order, Mr Gloag.' Fox stared hungrily down on to the maindeck. A rush was going to develop there any minute. Only the speed of events had held the French in a stasis. 'Prepare to

143

repel boarders.' The order sounded strange, even ridiculous; but Fox knew what he was doing.

He had a hand at the wheel, he had men in the maintop setting canvas—the French had probably removed the footropes up there to hinder just those actions; but a British topman could run out along the yard like a monkey in a circus—and he now had to deal with the French crew.

It was only when Gloag, fairly dancing with rage, pushed a dry pistol into Fox's ribs that he realised he was not in command, that he was a landsman lubber from a three-decker, that he had no position to endorse his order-giving.

'I'll shoot you, Fox! I'll cut you down! What the devil do you mean—?'

'Where were you when we boarded?' demanded Fox, the heat of the action still boiling in him. 'The ship is ours if we continue—' He brought his arm around, took the pistol away from Gloag and then, so suddenly the Scotsman flinched away from the priming, he lifted the pistol and shot through the first French head that appeared at the quarterdeck ladder. 'Here they come!'

He shoved Gloag aside, lifted the cutlass in his right hand—the shooting he had done with his left —and roared into the men who crowded up the ladder. The marines were shooting. British seamen pushed after him. He was in among the French; pistols banged, cutlasses clanged together like a tinker's convention, blood gouted from severed wrists and slashed faces; the charge of the French up the ladder, necessarily on a narrow front, was changed dramatically to a charge of the British downwards; in a welter of steel and blood the whole mêlée surged forward. And now the *Tigers* from the forecastle could join in. As the frigate glided away from the roadstead the French were tumbled forward and down the forehatch. The door was left open. Fox shouted a savage order to the marine sergeant.

'Keep firing down, sergeant! They'll likely get up to monkey business if you don't keep them occupied!'

A strange new sound was added to the din. A new fight had broken out below decks. Fox hurried back aft. Beneath the quarterdeck was a whole area he had not cleared of French. When he arrived he heard British oaths mingled with French imprecations. Pistols were going off everywhere. Some new element had been added to the fight; but he could not stop to worry over that now. The ship had to be navigated down the roadstead, past the boom, and out to the waiting *Poppy* and *Rosinante*.

There was something odd and strange about this frigate. *Narcissus*, her name. Yet her cut, details about her, little things, rang bells in Fox's mind. Yes, by God! He had it.

This was *Mortagne!*

He was taking the same ship again, taking her for the second time.

There was no space to stop and wonder. As the ship cleared and began to pick up way he was roaring for men to go aloft and set the foretopsail.

The driver would be necessary now to carry her out to sea with the bend in the channel with the wind over her larboard quarter.

The Fort was firing again now. They could see the frigate, up there from their lofty perch, and the big forty-two-pound shot were striking down into the water and rousing ghostly spouts. One carried the mizzen royal mast away and Fox roared men to hack away the wreckage as it trailed overside, the long lines confused and dangerous in the darkness.

The shouting and yelling from below could be attended to now. They got a jib out and Fox, looking ahead, could see the lightness as the clouds cleared, and he thought he could pick up the flick of sail from one of the waiting craft. But that shouting and uproar from below. . . .

Gloag stood to face him as he turned.

'I don't know what this is all about, Fox,' said Gloag, icy about the lips, his bloodied leg clearly giving him pain. 'But—'

'I think we had better see what that infernal noise below is, Mr Gloag. And I'll trouble you to have that wound of yours attended to.'

Gloag shook his head. It had all clearly been too much for him.

They went down to the aft companionway and heard shouts and yells, and then, unmistakably, the sound of honest English sea oaths.

At once understanding hit Fox.

'The British crew! Of course. They're battened down below—and we drove the French in on top

146

of 'em!' He threw his head back and laughed and the laugh was drowned in the smash of a forty-two pound ball into the counter.

'This is priceless!' said George Abercrombie Fox. He was a man who did not laugh often or easily; but when he did so he liked to let the laugh break free, to let his belly rumble and shake. And this, surely, was such a time for laughter.

When the doors were flung back a motley crowd bounded out on deck. British seamen wielding bits of wood, knives, captured cutlasses, they poured out ready to deal with the enemies they expected to meet.

'By God!' said Fox. 'I don't know who planned this night's attack; but the man was a dunder-headed fool! First the mess at the boom, and all surprise lost—and now this! Surely he must have known the British prisoners were still aboard!'

A figure stepped through the throng and the sea-men stood aside to let through the British captain. They did not, it seemed to Fox in that moment, look on their captain with any favour.

Gloag was burbling on as the newcomer approached.

'It is with great relief I see you are alive and well, sir,' Gloag was saying.

But Lord Lymm, he who had been as the hon-ourable Charles Beckworth, the bane of Fox's life, was glaring at that worthy as though at the risen dead.

'Mr Fox!' Lord Lymm said, his face and voice filled with the surprise he felt, a surprise no greater than that evinced by Gloag. 'Mr Fox! So *Duchess* had a hand in this!'

'No, sir,' Fox said. '*Tiger.*'

He made his explanations quickly and curtly. There was still a lot to do. A brisk series of splashes over the side told of the French crew jumping through the ports to swim to shore rather than be carried to the hell of a British prison hulk. The fort was still firing sullenly, but their aim was ragged now and with every yard *Narcissus* made the chance of being crippled receded. Now he would have to get the ship out past the boom, set watches, get things under control—he pulled himself up with a jerk. Once again he had forgotten that, as far as Gloag was concerned, he was just a landsman.

But Beckworth—he'd have to accustom himself to thinking of him as Lord Lymm now—and Gloag were talking together, and there was Haines, white-faced but evidently conscious of his lieutenant's uniform and status. Fox would have to let Lymm as the senior officer take over. He smiled his spiteful little smile to himself. That should prove interesting.

Gloag was standing before him now, his lugubrious face filled with wonder.

'If that doesn't beat all,' Gloag said. 'So it's Lieutenant Fox, after all. So you are a King's Officer!'

CHAPTER ELEVEN

The marine sentry standing stiffly at the door to the admiral's quarters let Lieutenant Fox past and, not without a tremor of an excitement he despised in himself, Fox went through the anteroom with its twelve-pounder burnished and shining and so into the aft cabin. The impression of light pouring in through the array of windows in the stern, the light-coloured paintwork, the fancy decorations, the pictures, the elegant tables and chairs, all the evident manifestations of opulence here had on him only the effect of increasing his hunger.

Vice-Admiral Sir Blundesely Creighton, seated at his desk, looked up as Fox entered. A mass of papers and documents covered the deak, and the secretary, a grey wisp of a man with ink stains behind his ears and a neck like a vulture's, regarded Fox with the distaste of a busy man unwarrantably interrupted in his work.

The flag captain, Sir John Pulteney, prowled the cabin on the larboard side, rounding the twelve-pounders, his lean bulk bent beneath the overhead, his sinewy hands clasped behind his back. Between him and the admiral the impression of broad blue cloth, white silk and the painful glitter of gold might have confused and awed a humble lieutenant dressed in nothing better for uniform than what the tailor of *Tiger* had cobbled together for him.

But Fox was in no mood to be impressed. He knew his place, for it ill-betided any man in this day and age to forget where he stood in the social structure; but he also remembered the incredible bungling of the attack on *Narcissus,* and the dead men as a consequence.

'Come in, come in, lieutenant.' The admiral pushed papers aside. He stared up at Fox challengingly. 'So you're the officer who was fool enough to be snatched by the press, egad! I don't know what the Service is coming to. I'd have broken a few heads if they'd done it to me, I can tell you, sir.'

'Yes, sir,' said Fox, dutifully.

The press gang would no doubt immediately and instinctively have recognised in this broad bluff man with the hectoring eyelids and the self-indulgent mouth a gentleman and an officer. If Creighton had protested as Fox had, they'd have believed him.

'Well, we got *Narcissus* back.' The admiral could take great comfort and pleasure from the thought. She was a fine frigate, re-rated in the Royal Navy as a thirty-six—the Frogs always over-sparred and over-gunned their ships—and the captain to whom she had been entrusted had sailed out of Plymouth and been snapped up like a fat trout biting on the first fly that came his way.

Some feelings of political rancour occurred to Admiral Creighton, for this Lord Lymm was a man of influence and active in the Government party's intrigues. Creighton could see that, else the noble Lord would never have been given a command; but it was a pointer to why the ship had been lost. Politics and the Navy were inextricably entwined, and there was no way of changing that that he could see.

Captain Pulteney gave a cough that was meant to remind his admiral that affairs awaited; Creighton couldn't stand his flag captain; it had been a mistake taking the feller in the first place. But there he was, duly appointed for the commission of *Tiger*. He shuffled papers and stabbed a glance at Fox.

'I have had despatches, Mr Fox. Some are about you. I have heard the story from Mr Gloag—you will be pleased to hear that his wound is mending nicely.'

'Yes, sir.'

'And I have read your report. You do not mince matters in your statements about the planning of the attack.'

'No, sir.'

Writing that report had given Fox a few nasty hours of indecision. In the end he had not compromised, and had criticised freely. He had cheated, though. He had been able to be much freer in his criticisms than he would normally have been purely because he had gone along as a simple seaman—a landsman, according to his rating. He had told of his experiences from the point of view of a man involved at lower deck level, apportioning blame to an amorphous higher authority without the necessity for naming names, for he did not know them, even if he could guess. He could not be censured for that.

Creighton tapped the paper.

'You will be sorry to learn that Lieutenant Shadwell, the officer who planned the attack, was killed.'

Fox inclined his head. 'I had heard, sir. I am truly sorry that such a fine officer has been lost to the Service.'

'A round shot splattered his head into fragments,' said Creighton, reflectively. He had not been there; but any naval officer could imagine that ghastly scene.

Captain Pulteney coughed again. Creighton glanced over at him, and then back.

'There was some talk of the Patriotic Fund voting you a sword of honour to the value of thirty pounds, Mr Fox.'

Fox's heart lurched. If he could wear a sword of honour—that would be a cachet not lightly come by. And he could always pawn it with some ship's chandler for supplies. . . .

'However, they took the view that as you did not hold an active commission aboard *Tiger,* the ship involved, and were not charged with the attack in a position of command, the regulations did not hold.' Creighton shuffled his papers again and Fox felt all his old hatred of authority and patronage swell like a black bilious sac in his throat. If that mordaunt tumour broke he might do anything stupid, do or say something that would ruin his career for ever. And with his career ruined he would ruin his family and condemn them to grinding poverty for the rest of their lives.

He forced himself to remain blank-faced. He said: 'Yes, sir. I understand sir.' They'd denied him a sword for his part in the taking of *Nuestro Señora del Salvator* over a technicality. Lloyd's Patriotic Fund presented swords of honour with money collected by public subscription; Fox could scarcely expect the citizens of London to subscribe to a sword for a Thames-side marshboy. 'And *Duchess*, sir?'

Creighton shook his head at once.

'You'll not be sent back to her, Mr Fox. Anyway, she's been transferred and is on special duty. That's her function, as you well know.'

'Yes, sir.'

At last Captain Pulteney could contain himself no longer. He had been unable to turn down command of a ninety-eight, such a course would have been as much the ruination of his career as a battle lost, but he heartily wished that Admiral Creighton would take himself off to some other ship. The love lost between the men rubbed off in the ship.

'I lost two officers cutting that damned frigate out,' he said, turning to face his admiral. 'With your permission, sir, I'd like to write Mr Fox into the books of *Tiger*.'

The admmiral permitted himself a tiny smile. He had made Pulteney actually ask for a favour, and that pleased him. Of course, it was the sensible thing to do, and if Pulteney had had any sense he would have realised the admiral would do it, and was only playing the captain along. Now Creighton could afford to be generous.

'Consider yourself fortunate, Mr Fox. The appointment to a ninety-eight is not come by lightly.' That was true, Fox knew well enough. 'And you will continue at full pay. There are precious few officers who don't have to go on half-pay between commissions, believe you me.'

All Creighton was doing here was rubbing salt into Pulteney's wounds. Fox could see the animosity flickering between these two men, and he didn't like it. He hated them both; but he felt they should be able to work in harmony for the sake of the Service, and for the men under their command. No wonder Shadwell, poor devil, had made such a botch of it.

He cleared his throat, and as though part of his answer to the admiral, said: 'Are there any letters for me, sir, among the despatches?'

'Letters?' Creighton looked vaguely at the littered desk. He glanced over at the secretary who had not left the room but, like a nibbling little mouse, had remained silently crouched in an aft corner on a locker.

'No letters for Mr Fox were aboard the cutter

from Plymouth, sir,' said the secretary, and his Adam's apple gobbled in his vulturine neck and he thoroughly enjoyed conveying this discomfiting piece of news to this arrogantly bumptious lieutenant.

'Thank you, sir,' said Fox. He kept his face, as always immobile; but a hint of mistiness, a tiny cincture of purple and black, surrounded his left eye.

His mother would dictate a letter to Susan, if she could, and his sister would see it was sent; the difficulty was knowing where to send it with despatch; Plymouth, at the moment his home port, had in this case not been honoured. And there was young Bert. Fox felt a strange and warming sensation flooding over him and for a second did not recognise it as pleasant remembrance; for thought of Bert brought up memories of Captain Rupert Colburn of the Forty-third regiment of foot. Rupert had taken young Bert under his wing and Fox supposed that the soldier cherished notions of affection for Fox that he was completely unaccustomed to receive from anyone outside the family.

If Captain Rupert Colburn could write to Fox, he would do so; Fox tried to think that he was not more disappointed at not hearing from Rupert than his mother. That couldn't be possible, of course: that he had even entertained a glimmer of thought that it might showed with what a different regard he held Captain Rupert Colburn from any other officer alive.

Captain Pulteney was regarding him with that

bilious look of disfavour that turned his face into that of a dyspeptic Saint Bernard. Yet the man was a womaniser, so Fox had heard. It wasn't the man that obtained his amatory conquest but his position, his influence, his money, Fox guessed, enviously.

'I fear you may encounter some—ah—difficulties, Mr Fox, in serving as an officer aboard a ship in which you have served as a seaman—'

Admiral Creighton interrupted. Admirals could do that. 'Nonsense, Captain Pulteney! Mr Fox seems quite capable of handling himself, I have no doubt.'

Fox allowed the hint of a pleased smile to spread on his face. The expression was required in response to an admiral's witticism or patronising flattery. Keeping a blank face when an admiral required a smile was just the same as smiling out of turn—it was all 'Silent Insubordination'.

He began to think that Creighton would invite him to dinner. It was commonly done. Admirals and captains asked their officers to dinner as a matter of form, a courtesy, and, in Fox's case, he had a tale to tell. Once he could claim their attention, make them believe that he was a supremely competent officer and, what was far more important, an extremely lucky officer, he would stand in the way of his promotion at last. He wouldn't mind being the admiral's favourite, being sent away on special tasks, getting all the interesting things to do. That was the way penniless young lieutenants greased the way for their step.

'Very well, Mr Fox,' said Admiral Creighton, picking up his papers. The secretary stirred from his locker and began to creep back to the desk. 'I'll compliment you again on what you have done. Taking the same ship twice is a rare accomplishment. You've made a promising start aboard. Now I'm sure Captain Pulteney—'

It was a dismissal.

Cold, matter of fact, a dismissal. No dinner. No further sweet words. He was being kicked out, as usual.

Pulteney said: 'Report to the first lieutenant, Mr Fox. I have an idea he can find a use for you on the lower gun deck.'

'Aye, aye, sir,' said Fox.

He gave them a sketchy salute and turned away, blundered out the door, past the marine sentry, and so out and into the fresh air of the Atlantic where the waves rolled in beneath *Tiger*'s larboard bow and rolled her up and down and roiled away from her starboard quarter. He took a deep breath. He was back to sea duty again. A lowly junior lieutenant subject to all the iron discipline of the Navy. Well, he was still alive. And there was some prize money for the family; not much, but enough for the time being, until something fresh hove up into his sights.

George Abercrombie Fox took a last look at the sea and sky and felt the wind on his cheek; then he dived below into the noisome stinks from the bilge to find his new duty on the lower gun deck.

157

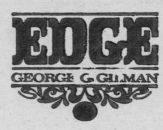